Antonio Manuel Fraga

TARTARUS

Published in 2018 by
SMALL STATIONS PRESS
20 Dimitar Manov Street, 1408 Sofia, Bulgaria
You can order books and contact the publisher at
www.smallstations.com

This book was first published in the Galician language as *Tártarus*
by Edicións Xerais de Galicia (Vigo, 2016). The series GALICIAN
WAVE: The Way of Fiction exists to showcase the best of Galician
young adult fiction in English. More information can be found at www.
smallstations.com/wave

*This work received a grant from the General Secretariat of Culture of the
Ministry of Culture, Education and University Planning of the Xunta de
Galicia in the call for translation grants of the year 2017*

*Esta obra recibiu unha axuda da Secretaría Xeral de Cultura da
Consellería de Cultura, Educación e Ordenación Universitaria da Xunta
de Galicia na convocatoria de axudas para a tradución do ano 2017*

ISBN 978-954-384-091-5

Antonio Manuel Fraga

TARTARUS

Translated from Galician by **Jonathan Dunne**

Small Stations Press

for my parents

Far safer, of a midnight meeting
External ghost,
Than an interior confronting
That whiter host.

Emily Dickinson, *Complete Poems*

And when he came to the place where the wild things are
they roared their terrible roars and gnashed their terrible teeth
and rolled their terrible eyes and showed their terrible claws.

Maurice Sendak, *Where the Wild Things Are*

*I*t was undoubtedly a pleasant coincidence to come across Mastrina's story again after all that time.

"Guiomar, I'm not telling you again, I swear I'll throw it all out!" my father had warned. So on my next visit to the old family home, I loaded the car with cardboard boxes containing a wide variety of relics from my past.

The old man had decided to sell the house. Ever since my mother's death, it had got too big for him. The news caught my brother and me by surprise, albeit we had to accept the reasons he expounded to us.

Back in the warmth of my apartment, I gazed in fascination at the contents of the boxes, remnants of the shipwreck of my distant childhood. There, in no particular order, was a whole bunch of stuff.

I patiently dedicated a whole Sunday afternoon to separating the valuable objects from the junk, even though there were times when the border between these two categories was rather difficult to discern.

In a shoebox, I found all the information that forms the basis of this text. Newspaper and magazine cuttings, photocopies from encyclopaedias, adverts, a recipe... everything I compiled back then to illustrate Mastrina's story, which I had taken down in teenage handwriting in a graph-paper notebook.

Unhurriedly, over a period of several months, I used my weekends to read, order and rewrite all the material.

Here is the result of that endeavour, which allowed me to relive with veritable pleasure an autumn that marked me much more than I could ever have suspected.

PART I

BRAGUNDE

LAW
FOR THE CREATION
OF NABRALLOS

* * * * * * *

Audierna's urban space will be divided into areas segregated by race. Members of the Brun community will only be able to live in nabrallos and will require a passport and work permit to leave these areas. The nabrallos will be created for the exclusive use of Audierna's Brun community. It will constitute a crime for any member of the Brun community to reside or own properties in areas reserved for the Gwende community.

It had rained constantly over the old quarter during those first few days of September, more than usual, and the streets had been varnished with this slippery, reddish film. That summer had been the hottest in memory and, with the sudden arrival of the cold, the dogs had abandoned the cool patches of shade in order to wander up and down the muddy streets.

At that time, Plugufan was already a place that was tired of its grandeur, an epic past that justified the decrepitude of its houses, which slouched lazily over their wrought-iron porches. People moved slowly up and down the streets. This was normal – only old folk lived in those parts. Ancient Gwendes slid along the pavements like snails, invariably dressed in clothes that were as unfashionable as the quarter itself. Those who weren't leaning on sticks or crutches advanced in wheelchairs being pushed resignedly by Brun maids dressed in black. Whenever two of these aged people encountered each other, they gently bowed their heads in respect. They then began a conversation that didn't normally surpass family and meteorological limits, which the Bruns would listen to, standing as stiff as their dark uniforms. Having exchanged a few words, they would then repeat their greeting and continue on their painful way.

This first visit to Mastrina's quarter had turned into an enforced journey to another age. It annoyed me having to walk along streets that were unpaved, long and narrow, laid out in a grid on the north bank of the River Ioke, and getting my new trainers and the bottoms of my trousers all dirty in the mud. It also annoyed me having to waste four hours a week banging away on a klavia. Why did my mother have to be so obsessed with details? That was her problem! If she hadn't pored over the newspaper every Sunday as if it was Holy Scripture, then perhaps she wouldn't have noticed that insignificant advertisement: "Klavia classes by Mastrina Xaoven, ex-director of the Audierna Philharmonic. Price by agreement. 221-B Bagare Street."

"Guiomar!" she had shouted enthusiastically from the garden the previous Sunday morning. It hadn't started raining yet, so she was breakfasting in the company of my father, who was reading another newspaper through his round glasses, guiding his reading with the tip of his left forefinger and twitching his moustache from time to time in inaudible whispers.

"Yes, mother!" I replied, appearing in the doorway of the house while hiding the water pistol I was using to battle my brother behind my back.

"Come here, girl, don't make me shout!"

I laid my weapon on the ground, next to the door, and lazily dragged my feet until I was standing behind her. I gently stroked her short hair. The morning light filtered through the branches of the sycamore in the garden, a huge parasol with grey, scaly bark. One day, I thought, I also shall have short hair, like all Gwende women. Until then, I would have to make do with tying my hair in a ponytail.

"Take a look at this, Guiomar. Do you know who this woman is?" she asked, so excited she even stopped her husband twitching his moustache.

"If she lives in Plugufan, I suppose she might be a mummy," I laughed, resting my chin on her shoulder in order to read the advert.

"Please be so good as to not be frivolous," she pretended to get annoyed. "Mastrina Xaoven directed the Philharmonic during its most glorious epoch. She is quite an eminence."

"I reckoned she was dead," remarked my father.

"She may well be," I joked again. "An advert from the other side."

"Stop fooling around!" my mother rebuked me, banging me on the head with the rolled-up newspaper. "It's about time you started taking the klavia seriously. We spent a whole load of money on that instrument."

"Artusa dusts it, covers it in cloths, gives it flowers… it must be her favourite piece of furniture." Artusa was the family's Brun maid. "Anyway, it's not the only artefact in the house."

I sat down between my parents and buttered a slice of toast. Out of the corner of my eye, I noticed my father's mocking smile, the sparkle of his grey eyes. My mother, on the other hand, was not laughing. She placed the newspaper on the table, right on top of a pool of orange juice, which was absorbed by the newspaper, smudging the black letters.

"This afternoon, your father and I will go to Bagare to talk to Mastrina. If possible, you will start classes next week. You know how important it is to complement your academic learning with the mastery of an instrument."

"You're not serious," I ventured, starting to get a little worried about the direction the conversation was taking.

"I most certainly am."

I glanced at my father with a supplicating look, but he hid his face behind the newspaper.

"In which case, when do I get to train with the team?"

"Guiomar Brelivete," my treacherous father remarked from his hiding place, "thirteen years old, average student, only worried about sport and expensive clothes. Little girl, it's about time you got a move on! When did you ever hear of somebody getting a place at Verrenorde University for being good at maila?"

"But the team needs me! You promised me another year!"

"Obligations take precedence over promises, daughter," murmured my mother, stroking my hand. "Two days a week, you will attend klavia classes, and another two days you can dedicate to your team."

"You'd worked this out beforehand!" I accused them.

"I think it's only fair."

"Fair in your opinion!" I exclaimed, pulling my hand away. I jumped to my feet and ran into the house. The tears were streaming down my cheeks, and I was choked with rage.

When I entered the living room, I got a jet of water from my brother's water pistol right in the face.

"Are you an idiot, or what?" I shouted, dealing him a hefty slap.

I immediately realized my mistake and tried to say sorry, but it was too late. He stared at me in anger for a couple of seconds and then went to tell my parents. I spent the rest of the day being punished in my bedroom and pondering my misfortune. I hated the klavia, and all music in general. I also hated this stupid, old woman who had placed the advertisement, even before I'd had a chance to meet her.

My mother liked music just about as much as me, though she would go crazy with joy whenever my father got tickets from work for a performance. She loved this kind of occasion, which enabled her to show off her finest jewels and to dress her compliant husband up as a clown. In the corridors of the concert hall, they would rub shoulders with some of the most illustrious names in Audierna. It was rare for my brother and me to go with them. Tickets were extremely expensive, and my father only usually got a couple. Even so, when we did have to go, we would venture forth like a pig to the slaughter, my mother elbowing us in the ribs to make us greet everybody politely.

"221-B Bagare Street." That was the address, but the property didn't match the mental image I'd created for myself of the home of an ex-director of the Philharmonic. To start with, it didn't even border the street, but was hidden behind an old ironmonger's that seemed to have shut down years ago.

The house was narrow, with a small porch at the entrance and blue shutters on the windows. Its walls were an odd assortment of white planks warped by time and humidity. The front of the upper floor was entirely taken up by an enclosed balcony, the glass panes of which were caressed by the long fingers of a twisted oak. The railings were covered in colourful plant pots.

I trudged angrily up the steps to the porch and observed my mud-bespattered shoes. Pausing for a moment, I decided to press the bell, which echoed inside the house with a metallic moan. There was no answer. I checked on my watch that it was five past six in the evening, so I wasn't early. I waited a couple of seconds and tried the bell again. When the metallic sound had receded for a second time, I heard footsteps approaching the door. A bolt was drawn back, and a crack appeared between the door and the jamb.

"Yes?" asked an old woman's hoarse voice.

"Good evening. My name is Guiomar Brelivete. I'm here to learn the klavia. I think my parents have already spoken to you…"

"Ah, yes!" replied the voice, taking stock of the situation. "Come in, come in."

The woman opened the door wide and waited for me to enter the hallway.

"Follow me," she indicated.

We climbed a staircase covered in a maroon carpet that

creaked under our feet. The air was thick and smelled of mould. For a moment, I felt sick.

At the top of the staircase was a large, rectangular room with a white klavia in the centre. The soft evening light came flooding in from the balcony, unhindered by curtains tied to both sides of an arch that connected the two spaces.

In the opposite wall, a small window revealed the darkness in the east. It occupied the only gap left by shelves that lined the walls, crammed full of books, records and magazines. At the bottom of the bookcases were little doors with golden keys in their locks, from which hung maroon tassels. Some pictures were propped on the floor, and a single photograph took pride of place on the bookcase, next to an old record player. A thin, worn, brightly-coloured carpet covered the wooden floor. To complete the furniture, there was a rocking chair with a wicker back and a round table with a lamp.

The old woman sat in the rocking chair and looked me up and down. She was all bones set at awkward angles and had a slight squint in her left eye. She wore a green pinafore that revealed the lower part of her legs, two knobbly sticks deformed by ridges of varicose veins. She had long hair, which she wore down, something unusual in Gwende women of her age, and the lank, white locks slid over her shoulders.

As we gazed at each other in silence, I discovered a large, furry mass glistening in the evening sun in one corner of the balcony. Three cats were asleep, curled up in a knotted, ginger embrace.

"Your mother tells me you studied the klavia for three

years," the old woman finally commented.

"Yes, but not very regularly."

"Explain that to me."

"I missed a whole bunch of classes, and I never play at home. I'm a hopeless case, you see. I wish to make one thing clear: I hate the klavia. I hate it with all my strength. I'm here because my parents force me, and the days I spend banging away on this awful instrument are training sessions I'm going to miss with my team."

"What do you play?"

"Maila."

"Are you any good?"

"I'm not bad."

"I see…" mused the old woman. "Sometimes the passions choose us, and not the other way round. That happened to me with the klavia, and to you with sport. Come here for a moment."

She grabbed my hands and examined them closely.

"You've a quarryman's hands," she remarked. "What was the last thing you learned?"

"*Confederation of Honour and Bravery*, by Hervé."

"Are they still teaching that old rubbish? What a state we're in…"

She got out of the rocking chair with some difficulty and headed towards the stairs, dragging her feet.

"Sit on the klavia stool and wait for me," she barked. "We'll begin in a moment."

I stood in the middle of the room like an idiot, not knowing what to do. I decided to ignore her command and went over to the shelves that lined the walls. There were piles of books, mostly by authors I had never heard of. Most of the shelves, however, were covered in vinyl records. I was amazed to see they were almost all old hicupé records. I pulled one from the tightly-packed row and examined the ugly, strident cover that showed two Brun men dressed in dark suits and ties. They were both smiling, revealing large, white teeth, and each holding an instrument in their hands: a malgrine and a litenklave. Their hair was shaved at the sides and a little longer in the middle, and combed back with gel. I put the record back in the row and carried on inspecting the contents of the shelves. In front of the records and books, on the empty wooden surface, other objects were dotted about: the statuette of some prize, postcards of different destinations, their colours faded by the light, a charcoal drawing of some grazing sheep, an old camera… My attention was drawn to the only photograph, which was protected by an ornate silver frame that contrasted with the simple nature of the other objects. I took it from the shelf and wiped the glass on the sleeve of my jersey. It was a studio portrait, showing a handsome young man in his early twenties. Despite the absence of colour, I could make out his clear eyes. An ironic smile flickered on his lips, and he wore a military cap shunted to one side and what looked like a thick coat that must also have been army issue.

"Well, whaddya know?" I murmured in amusement, gazing at the young man. "She kept that quiet, didn't she?"

It was then I heard heavy breathing, close to suffocation, coming from behind me. I turned around and saw the old woman's face, which was pale and distorted by anger. I was so afraid I let go of the photograph, and it fell on the carpet, the glass smashing into a thousand tiny pieces.

"Oh my goodness, I'm so sorry!" I excused myself, bending down to pick up the pieces.

"Leave that alone!" roared the old woman. "Didn't I tell you to sit down! Who on earth gave you permission to go fiddling about!"

"I said I was sorry!" I countered forcefully.

"I said I was sorry, Mastrina Xaoven!" she corrected me.

I placed the tiny pieces on top of the shelf and with red cheeks tried to avoid looking the old woman in the eye.

"Let's get two things clear," she said while sitting down in the rocking chair. "First of all, you will address me as Mastrina Xaoven, at all times. Second, inside this house you will always do what I tell you. If you're not prepared to abide by these rules, or simply think you're not capable, then I ask you not to waste any more of your time, or mine. You know where the door is, don't you?"

I bit hard on my lower lip in an effort to overcome my rage and sense of impotence. How dare the old hag talk to me like that? If she was so damn fond of that photograph, then she should have kept it in a security box with a dozen locks and buried it in the garden. My first impulse was to raise my middle finger and get the hell out of there, but the fear of never being able to play maila again held me back. I swallowed my pride and lowered my head, hiding my face behind my blond locks.

"I'm truly sorry, Mastrina Xaoven," I muttered between gritted teeth. "I'm very clumsy."

"I'm not surprised, with fingers like those," smiled the old witch. "Now sit down at the klavia and play something."

I perched my bottom on the stool and lifted the klavia lid.

"What shall I play?"

"Anything. That nonsense by Hervé you mentioned earlier, for example."

I cracked my knuckles, as I'd seen my previous teacher do so often, and played the beginning of *Confederation of Honour and Bravery*. I got a couple of notes wrong, but to my amazement my interpretation of the piece wasn't too bad. Mastrina, judging by her wooden features, didn't seem to share my enthusiasm.

"You played the easiest part," she observed.

"I know. It's the part I like best."

"If you liked it, you wouldn't mess it up like that," she stated firmly. "Play the end of the piece, where it goes la-di-da-di-da…"

Suddenly a loud groan drowned out the old woman's command, and she grabbed her stomach in a gesture of pain. She instinctively huddled into a ball, placing her feet on the chair and throwing her head backwards. For a moment, she reminded me of the mummies on the third floor of the Natural History Museum, all doubled up and dry, all skin and wrinkles.

An itinerant cloud captured the last rays of the day. When it released them again, they entered from the balcony, revealing a thick atmosphere of dust. Time had ground to a halt after the old woman's groan. I was petrified, stock-still, looking at her without knowing what to do. Was she dying? I'd never seen a dead person before, and the day had already been sufficiently unpleasant not to want to have to endure that kind of experience as well!

"Are you OK, Mastrina?" I reacted finally, kneeling down in front of her.

"What do you think?" she asked in a broken voice. "Don't worry, these aches and pains and I are old friends. Please, Guiomar, would you go down to the kitchen and bring me a glass of water?"

"Where is the kitchen?"

"It's the first door on the right. There should be a glass next to the sink."

Despite the calmness with which she pronounced these words, I ran downstairs as if the old woman's life depended on my diligence. I found the glass where she had said and filled it with water. One of the ginger cats had followed me to the kitchen, and started yawning in the doorway. It then proceeded to clean its body with protracted licks. To return to the hallway, I had to jump over it.

When I handed her the glass, Mastrina pulled a jar of medication from the pocket of her pinafore. She took out a green pill, which she washed down with water. She then leaned back and closed her eyes, breathing deeply.

"Would you do me another favour? Take one of the records on the top shelves and put it on the turntable."

"Which would you like? There are thousands of them."

"I don't mind, any one will do."

I looked for the old hicupé record I had seen before, the one with the two Brun men smiling on the cover. When I found it, I took it out of its sleeve and placed it on the turntable. The contact of the needle with the vinyl produced a slight crackling on the speakers. Then the music began: first a drum roll that gradually grew in intensity.

"Strange choice!" affirmed the old lady.

The broken lament of a litenklave echoed around the room. The music rose and fell in an overwhelming torrent of notes until it stopped suddenly in a loud outburst that sounded like a challenge, a careful provocation. Then, almost without a pause, the malgrine entered the fray, spitting out musical reproaches at a dizzying pace. In the background, the percussionist continued banging away on the skin of the drums like a madman, inciting the duellists not to stop fighting until blood had dropped like a new seed on the ground. I'd never heard anything like it! What did this have in common with Hervé's boring, conceited compositions?

"Amazing, those two brothers," said Mastrina. "They were probably the most talented musicians of their generation, but they misspent their talent in bars and brawls. They recorded a couple of records and then vanished forever."

I involuntarily started tapping my feet in time to the music. This made Mastrina smile, and I smiled also.

"If you taught me Brun music, I wouldn't hate the klavia so much," I said without thinking.

"If I taught you such music, I don't think your parents would be all too happy. And please, don't use that term in front of me again."

"What term?"

"Brun. It's offensive," she declared severely. "What we're listening to is Malluma music, a culture that inhabited these lands when our own ancestors were starving to death in the north."

"Malluma?" I said in surprise. "Only they use that term."

"I'm a Gwende and I do as well. And from now on, I expect you to do the same, at least in this house."

I sat down on the carpet, crossing my legs. We listened in silence until the song ended.

"Mastrina Xaoven, can I ask something?"

"Go ahead."

"The man in the photograph, is he your son?"

"I never had any children," a sorrowful shadow flitted across her face.

"Your husband then?"

"No."

"Were you never married?"

"I was, many years ago. But you're not here to write my memoirs, so enough of that," she interrupted me before rising to her feet and approaching the klavia with difficulty. She gazed at the instrument and stroked the shiny, porcelain-white wood.

"If you hate her, she'll hate you as well," she affirmed, sitting down in front of the keyboard. "You have to learn to coexist, or this will be painful for all concerned."

She pressed the keys and started playing an old hicupé at a slower pace than that of the crazy dialogue on the record. I accompanied the music by whistling softly. I knew this melody, you bet I did! I'd heard Artusa humming it a thousand times while doing the cooking.

"When I was young," began Mastrina, playing all the while, "lots of young Gwendes ignored the security measures and visited the nabrallos to listen to hicupé."

"That's not possible! My father's always saying how difficult it was to get there!" I exclaimed from the carpet, rubbing the back of the cat that had followed me to the kitchen. Its companions remained in a ball on the balcony.

"It most certainly was!" laughed the old lady, picking up speed. "And yet, despite the complicated nature of the endeavour, many fans of this music risked making the journey. Getting to Bragunde was especially difficult, but it was worth it, that's where the best hicupé clubs were."

"Have you... have you ever been to the nabrallos?" I asked in fascination.

Mastrina stopped playing and turned the stool towards me.

"Me? I wish I had," she replied bitterly. "I was never brave enough for such adventures."

Old Xaoven seemed to glimpse the disappointment on my face, so she went on the counter-attack.

"Do you like stories?" she asked. Sparks of light flashed in her green eyes.

"I sure do. Like everybody, I suppose. Why do you ask?"

"I want to propose a deal: we'll divide your class time into two parts. If you invest a minimum amount of effort in learning to play the klavia, I'll tell you a story – a good one, too. It's about a girl just like you, perhaps a tiny bit older. It begins on the day she went to one of those clubs in the nabrallos. I think you'll like it."

The matter was clear: I either had to sit for two hours in front of the hated klavia or do so for less time and put up with the old woman's ravings. It didn't take me long to make up my mind.

"I like stories with magic in them," I confessed.

"Oh, this one has plenty..."

Karatengue's Freedom Ignites Protests in the Nabrallos

[Newspaper staff]

The officer from the SAN (Special Agency for the Nabrallos) was declared innocent of shooting and killing the Brun teenager Dimasus Lopo last February by arguing that he had acted in self-defence. His acquittal was met with demonstrations in the nabrallos, which turned violent in Bragunde, where Dimasus was from.

many cases to be about to

Autumn that year got off to an icy start. Not even the most experienced members of our community, however hard they tried, could find a precedent for such temperatures. My father said he couldn't remember such a cool September in all his life. And I believed him. This strange wind from the north licked the city with its tongue of inhospitable cold.

The northern blast caught the administrators of my school by surprise – they had yet to fill the two rusty heating tanks with fuel. Until the fuel company came to fill them again, we pupils and teachers were colder than sparrows in the classrooms.

And yet the cold wasn't the reason for my bad temper on the afternoon of my second visit to the house in Plugufan. As normal when I was leaving school, I had sat on the wall by the playground to wait for Nivardo, my neighbour. Ever since my first day at school, we had always walked home together after classes. I was sitting there like an idiot for about twenty minutes until the janitor locked the large, metal gate, thus confirming that the building was now empty.

What had happened? In all those years, Nivardo had never missed our daily meeting, except when he was operated on for appendicitis. We would wander slowly towards our street, catching up on the latest school news. Nivardo always knew all the latest gossip. If some teacher was hitting the bottle, or the janitor was flicking through naughty magazines, or this girl was dating that boy...

Nivardo would know about it. And he told it all with the most amazing sense of humour. I never laughed so much as when I was with him. I don't know whether it was just that I found him very funny, or puberty was messing about with my senses.

Despite being only three months older than me, Nivardo was one class above me because he'd been born in December and I'd been born in February. He was, above all, gorgeous to look at. Tall as a pine, with these broad shoulders, he looked older than his classmates. He hid his eyes behind a flop of blond hair, which he was always blowing out of the way, making this awkward gesture with his mouth. That way of twisting his lips would have looked ridiculous on the ugly, bespotted face of any other teenager, but not on Nivardo. Every blast of air that served to sway his golden locks augmented his good looks – and his ego – a tiny fraction more. So it was hardly surprising that half the girls in school had set their sights on him.

I can remember, even after all these years, how my blood boiled that afternoon. Worried about him, I ran towards our street, overtaking several groups of students milling around the northern quarters with their carefree conversations. When I turned from Alane Street on to 15 August Avenue, I saw him, and the sight froze my blood. Nivardo was walking along the boulevard with this new girl, Deidre Something, who'd arrived at school that same year from some town in the east. My fun companion had dumped me for that hag with the fat lips and ugly features! I would never forgive him! Watching his forefinger dancing up and down the little witch's back was more than I could bear.

I decided to alter my normal route so I wouldn't have to contemplate the two lovebirds and headed straight for Mastrina's house. Despite the raging cold, I was as hot as a firebrand when I got there. Just as on the first day, I had to press the bell twice before any sign of life emanated from indoors. The tiny head of one of the ginger cats gazed at me from the windowsill downstairs. It had a pink spot on its face, which enabled me to recognize the cat that had accompanied me to the kitchen on my first visit. When the door opened, it was already rubbing up against Mastrina Xaoven's legs.

"Good afternoon, Guiomar," the old woman greeted me with hands full of earth. "Excuse the delay, I was just rummaging about in the garden. You're a little early, aren't you?"

Mastrina asked me to wait upstairs and headed to the bathroom. From the klavia room, I could hear the sound of the tap in the washbasin. A couple of minutes later, the old woman entered the room from the stairs. She'd draped a black, woollen cardigan over her shoulders, the sleeves hanging limply at her sides.

"What are you doing on your feet? Sit down at the klavia," she ordered.

"What about the story?"

"Afterwards."

In disappointment, I dragged my feet over the carpet and sat down in front of the instrument. The wind was shaking the branches of the old oak tree opposite the balcony. Suddenly a heavy downpour landed on top of the roof.

"Shit!" I protested. "Now it's raining too! Will nothing go well for me today?"

"Watch your tongue, Guiomar," Mastrina rebuked me. "If it rains, let it rain, we're quite dry in here."

"But I didn't bring an umbrella!"

The old woman sat in the rocking chair and looked at me with a smile.

"In which case, I'll lend you one, what's the problem?" she declared.

I yanked up the klavia lid. I was angry and uncomfortable. The house stank of damp and cooked cabbage. I could feel the stench impregnating me with its sickly sweetness. Great, I thought, and now I'm going to smell of Brun cooking...

I passed the tip of my forefinger over the keys and pressed C. The note roused the two cats on the balcony, who stretched and headed slowly in the direction of Mastrina's feet, where they collapsed once more. The lively one with the pink spot wasn't in the room, so I guessed it had stayed downstairs.

"Are you going to tell me?" asked Mastrina abruptly.

"Tell you what?"

"What's going on. If your head is in the clouds, then this class isn't going to be much help."

I played another note – F this time – without taking my eyes off the klavia.

"It's nothing," I attempted to smile, but managed only an embittered grimace. "Teenage stuff, you know."

"Affecting all teenagers, or one in particular?"

I rotated the stool so I could look at the old lady, who was stroking the cats' backs with the sole of her slipper. She smiled.

"I don't feel comfortable talking to you about this."

"And I don't feel comfortable listening to you, so get it over with."

"OK then! This dumbass stood me up. I know it's stupid, we're not even going out. It's just that he used to accompany me home every day, and I'm annoyed he's gone off with somebody else without telling me."

At this point, I was afraid the old woman would burst out laughing, but that didn't happen.

"Nothing would change even if he did tell you," she declared seriously.

She got up from the rocking chair and scanned the records on the shelves. When she found what she was looking for, she took it out with the tip of her finger.

"Well, that's a coincidence," she mused enigmatically while placing the needle in the black groove of the vinyl. "I suppose it must mean something."

"I'm afraid I don't know what you're talking about."

She sat back down in the chair, and one of the cats leaped on to her lap. The deep sound of a motlave introduced a piece being played at normal speed.

"We're listening to The Colonels of Rhythm. This band and a scruffy boy were the sparks that ignited the fire of this story…"

In Bragunde Station, the day was drawing to a close. The hoarse loudspeaker announced the arrival of a new train in the distance, coming from the districts north of the river. When the weary travellers started getting off the carriages, an impassable cordon of SAN agents had already taken control of the platform. They formed two lines, the ones behind holding on to fierce bulldogs that foamed at the mouth. The strong beams of the spotlights blinded the passengers. Every now and then, the monotonous murmur of the station was interrupted by a siren from outside.

Attica descended on to the platform, hidden among the flock of people. Her hair was covered by the hood of her coat, so it couldn't be seen she was a Gwende. She wasn't the only one to do this. In among the battalion of weary bodies, lots of other Gwendes were camouflaged beneath the clothing typically associated with the nabrallos.

It was Attica's first visit to Bragunde, and she hoped the money she'd paid on the black market for a train ticket would be worth it. A shiver of fear ran down her spine as she sensed the agents' shadows behind the spotlights, and she noticed how her lower back had become drenched in warm sweat.

Despite the fact it wasn't cold at all, her body had started to tremble as soon as she'd got out of the carriage. She'd spent the forty-minute journey in silence, staring at the thick-soled boots that, together with the overcoat, the tight, three-quarter-length trousers and checked flannel shirt, completed her disguise as a Malluma girl.

The flock advanced slowly. Attica gripped the piece of paper in her pocket with instructions on how to reach the club. The sweat of her hands had smudged the letters, but it didn't matter, she knew the directions by heart. She knew, just as Olaf had explained to her, that the SAN agents wouldn't carry out controls on people arriving on trains between six and eight in the evening. In those two hours, most of the battalion of workers who travelled to Gwende districts to work would be returning to the nabrallos. Bricklayer's mates, cooks, waiters, cleaners... a whole army of cheap labour. Far too many people to identify one by one.

Shaking, she crossed the police cordon, feeling the nervous breath of one of the bloodhounds on her neck. Attica also knew, when she got out of the station, she would have to turn left, walk two hundred yards along a broad avenue, cross the road and enter an alleyway called Crossing-76.

Despite looking like a bombed-out city, Bragunde smelled of the fruit and vegetables that were heaped up on roadside stalls. Attica advanced along the nabrallo's main avenue, which ran parallel to the railway. In amazement, she tried to engrave each photograph of the evening on her retina. In her desire to take everything in, she didn't notice the presence of an enormous hole at her feet and almost fell in because her head was in the clouds.

The astonishing vitality of the people in Bragunde was in stark contrast to the decrepitude of the buildings, which seemed in many cases to be about to collapse in a cloud of dust. Over the streets, designed with a set square by Gwende technicians, hung white sheets from the balconies, arrogant flags drying in the sun. The open lids of sewers, another danger that needed to be taken into consideration, occasionally expelled fetid burps, forcing passers-by to cover their mouths.

She worked out she must have gone two hundred yards, so she scrunched up her eyes to see the sign that gave the alleyway on the other side of the avenue its name: "Crossing-76." That was it! But now she was faced by another problem: how to dodge the nabrallo's chaotic traffic and make it safely over the broad avenue? Hundreds of vehicles stood between the girl and her objective, old cars that were no longer suitable for Gwende districts, noisy motorbikes, horses and carts, bikes... none of which seemed to obey any kind of logic.

Attica observed a group of hoodies crossing the avenue ten

yards in front of her. She deduced they were probably Gwendes heading to the club, so she copied their determination and stepped on to the tarmac. She jumped from place to place, dodging obstacles and ignoring car horns. When she reached the other side, she was sweating from stress and had a strange tingling sensation in her fingers.

She caught her breath and entered the alley. Dozens of young people were sheltering in the calm of the street, huddled in animated conversation. Their ages ranged from thirteen or fourteen to thirty something. Attica, who had already turned sixteen, was among the youngest.

Some still had their hoods up, but most had taken them off. Everybody, without exception, was wearing a long, green overcoat just like hers.

The club's facade was made of blackened bricks that were almost completely papered over at the bottom by layer upon layer of old posters. On each side of the main entrance, two twisted columns tried to give the building a pretty appearance, while, perched on top of the roof, two cement eagles kept an eye on the street. On their breasts, in sculpted letters, could be seen the name of the club and the year of its foundation.

Attica approached the ticket window and bought two tickets. She'd arranged with Olaf that the first to arrive would do this and then wait for the other next to the entrance. Attica had been confident her friend would be there and immediately felt uneasy on noticing his absence. There was still half an hour to go before the concert, however, so she endeavoured to remain calm.

While waiting, she amused herself watching this little urchin who, by shouting out to onlookers, had succeeded in gathering quite a large group of spectators.

"Ladies and gentlemen," roared the ragamuffin. "Come closer

if you would like to contemplate the unseen, the incredible, the amazing, the fearless child with the iron feet!"

The loudmouth, Attica reckoned, couldn't be more than twelve. He wore light grey trousers with patches and a green, woollen jumper that was far too big for his minuscule body. He had curly, overlong hair, and the skin of his face was so dark it looked as if it had never come into contact with water. He was holding a metal bucket in one hand, which he held out to his audience from time to time to show them what was inside.

"Embers! White-hot, burning coals! Who would like to reach out their hand and confirm how hot they are? You, my beautiful lady? Or perhaps you, brave sir?"

The huddled onlookers laughed at his exaggerated speech, and from time to time somebody would reach out their hand in response to his request.

"Now, please step backwards. I am going to empty the contents of this bucket on the ground, and I wouldn't want anyone to get hurt!"

He scattered the embers on the tarmac, creating an ashen walkway with reddish glowing spots. Then, very ceremoniously, he took off his shoes and hitched his trousers up to his knees. The boy stood at one end of the walkway and closed his eyes in concentration. The expectation of the audience increased, and little by little the conversations petered out.

From her position, Attica observed a curious phenomenon with amusement: dodging in and out of the expectant audience, a couple of other ragamuffins were checking the pockets of all those present. Suddenly, however, a Malluma boy cottoned on to the trick.

"Hey, what are you doing?" he shouted while trying to catch the thief.

"We're being robbed!" said a Gwende girl accusingly, pointing at the pair of pickpockets.

The would-be fakir, now that the game was up, gave the embers a hearty kick with his bare foot, raising an annoying cloud of dust that forced those present to protect their eyes. When they finally managed to open them again, the three bandits were already legging it out of the alleyway.

The young people were all checking whether they'd been robbed or not when the club opened its doors, causing an avalanche in its direction. Attica waited another ten minutes, alone in the queue, before having to admit that Olaf wasn't coming. Her first thought was to get out of there, but then she decided the best thing was to make the most of her ticket.

She entered the club and climbed some narrow stairs to the top gallery. There, sheltered in the dark, the Gwendes who'd made the secret journey from the north of the city to attend the concert waited expectantly.

Attica left her coat in the cloakroom and combed her blond hair with her hands, trying to give it some shape after it had been squashed under her hood for hours. It was short at the sides and longer in the middle, the straight locks falling to the right in such a way that one of her ears was hidden while the other, adorned with three rings, was left in the open. Another ring, small and golden, hung between her nostrils.

She leaned over the balcony of the gallery. A mass of sweating bodies swayed from side to side down in the orchestra. Dark looks were being aimed at the curtains that hid the stage. They had just started whistling at the delay when the curtains slid to the sides, eliciting a whoop of joy. A quartet stood on the stage, smiling at the audience. Once the shouting had died down, the musicians headed towards their places. At the front, closest to the public, were the two players of wind instruments, a malgrine and a litenklave. On the right, the klavia player sat in front of his black instrument, while the percussionist, the youngest of the four, disappeared behind a huge drum set located at the back of the stage.

The concert got off to a rumbustious start. The boy on drums set a lively rhythm, which the rest of the group followed in a swift and artful piece. Attica kept time with her feet, and a smile of pure happiness radiated across her face. She couldn't take her eyes off the klavia player's fingers, which swept up and down the keys like a murmuration of starlings on a snowy landscape.

Down in the orchestra, dozens of couples had formed, dancing spasmodically to the rhythm of the furious hicupé. The heat increased, the air got thicker and thicker. The dancers gradually divested themselves of articles of clothing until lots of boys were naked from the waist upwards. It was the girls who, rolling their eyes, led their partners. They had their sleeves rolled up and their necklines lower than was even imaginable in districts of the north. But this wasn't the boring north! This was a nabrallo, and this was the sound it made.

The dark skins shone under a varnish of sweat, in a collective trance that had Attica floating until the music faded away. For the girl, the concert lasted no longer than a flash of lightning, and she exited the club, feeling drugged by an exultant sense of happiness.

As she stepped outside, she felt something crunching under the thick sole of her boot, as if she'd trodden on a dry reed. She lifted her foot and saw she'd crushed a scorpion with a red body and yellow legs. She looked around and discovered there was a long line of these insects marching down the alleyway from the avenue and disappearing down a drain. From time to time, someone would notice their presence and scream in alarm or contempt. Attica covered her head with the hood of her coat and headed back to the avenue. There, she found other lines of scorpions skittering across the tarmac. She shivered in disgust and hurried towards the station.

As she passed in front of one of the alleyways that branched off the main avenue, she heard a boy whining and then pleading with somebody. Curiosity overcame her fear, and she ended up going down the alley, which was lit only by a street lamp with broken glass.

Against the wall that closed off the exit, she perceived the silhouettes of two SAN agents. One of them was holding a tiny, little boy under the arms while the other shouted at him in a threatening voice. Attica was just about to get the hell out of there when one of the agents gave the boy a slap that sent his face flying backwards. A yelp of pain filled the alley.

Some instinct sprouted in the girl's insides, causing her to run at the group and push the bully who'd beaten the boy against the wall.

"Damn brute!" she chastised him.

The agent, shielded by his armour, hardly registered the shove. He gazed at her in amusement for a couple of seconds, then punched her violently on the temple. Attica fell to the ground. Her head started spinning. When she came to, she noticed the back of her assailant's leg was unprotected. In a rage, she ran towards him and sank her teeth into his calf, causing him to shout in agony.

The other agent released the boy and gave Attica a brutal kick in the stomach, which made her lose her vision for a few moments. The girl crouched down on the ground like a wounded animal. One of the men bent down next to her and removed her hood.

"Shit!" he exclaimed in consternation. "It's a Gwende!"

The little boy used this moment of confusion to escape along the avenue, and one of the agents went running after him.

Attica's head gradually emerged from the eddy the kick had thrown it into, and she recovered her sight. Near her, she could see the leather boots of one of the agents, who was staring in confusion at another long line of scorpions on the ground. She noticed a thick stake not far away, probably the remnants of some old shed. She looked up carefully and saw the man had taken off his helmet, which was dangling in his hands.

Attica weighed up her strength. Her head was pounding, and the pressure in her stomach made it difficult to breathe. She closed her eyes and counted to three before grabbing the stick, jumping up and bringing it down on the man's head with all her might. The agent crumpled to his knees, out of action, and felt the blood soaking his scalp with the palm of his hand.

The girl dropped the stake and rushed towards the exit. As she turned the corner, back on the avenue, she came across a group of ten SAN agents who, having heard their colleague's shouts from the end of the alley, started to pursue her. As soon as she could, Attica turned left and entered a maze of gloomy streets. As she raced along, she had to dodge groups of Mallumas playing cards on little tables set out on the pavement, enjoying the pleasant evening temperatures. The players interrupted their games for a moment to observe the chase before quickly going back to the rumpus of their matches. Attica could hear the threatening, trampling sound of the agents' boots behind her, mixed with the odd shout ordering her to halt.

Having turned again, she heard a familiar voice calling to her. It came from inside this little shack with boarded-up windows.

"Hey, Chiona! This way!!"

Without thinking twice, she raced into the building, from the ceiling of which hung a rope. With the little energy she had left, she climbed the rope to a dark hole in between the boards. On the upper floor, she instinctively lay down on the rotten wood and pulled up the rope. The darkness stank of urine. Through a crack, she could see two lights examining the basement. The agents with the torches walked slowly, illuminating piles of rubble scattered across the floor.

"You sure she hid in here?" asked a female voice.

"Not exactly," replied a man. "She disappeared when she turned the corner. It's just a possibility."

Attica held her breath. The guards' movements mingled with the racket of the card games, which continued out on the street as if nothing had happened.

"This place is full of bugs!" complained the man.

"You don't say!" answered the woman ironically. "In a nabrallo? Now, there's a surprise!"

A shaft of light filtered through the boards for a moment, and Attica saw this enormous pair of eyes gazing at her in the darkness.

She then felt something moving near her hand and quickly pulled it back. In the darkness, she could make out the shape of several scorpions scampering over the floor, looking for an exit. Fear clambered up her throat, and she had to put her hand on her mouth to stifle a scream■

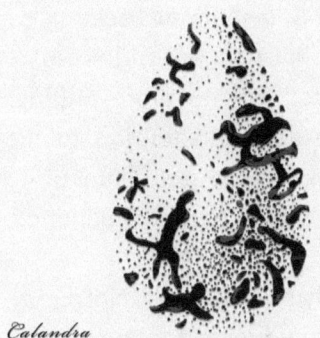

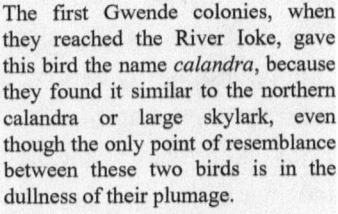

The first Gwende colonies, when they reached the River Ioke, gave this bird the name *calandra*, because they found it similar to the northern calandra or large skylark, even though the only point of resemblance between these two birds is in the dullness of their plumage.

The calandra's harmonious song is made up of many different notes, which are never repeated twice in succession in the same order. An unusual characteristic of the calandra is its ability to imitate the song of other birds, which it reproduces with slight variations.

Calandra

"And that's the end of the story for today," concluded Mastrina, checking the time on a watch she kept in the pocket of her pinafore.

"Already?" I replied, annoyed at the interruption.

"Yes."

I then spoke without thinking. It didn't take me long to regret this decision.

"But didn't you say the story was going to have some magic in it? It's been a bit on the weak side so far…"

Whoever said such a thing? Mastrina got up from the rocking chair with unusual violence for someone of her age and physical condition, forcing the cat on her lap to gambol through the air so as not to land on its back.

"You young people today!" snorted the old woman. "Ungrateful wretch… Well, that's it, no more talking, from now on we shall devote all our attention to the klavia. Let's see if you can manage to play something without bursting my eardrums! Not an ounce of patience, goodness me, not an ounce."

I was taken aback by the old lady's sudden fury. Not daring to look her in the eyes, I raced downstairs and emerged on to the street. I didn't stop running until I got home.

"How did it go with your new teacher?" asked my mother when she saw me coming in through the door.

"Pff, I couldn't tell you…"

"What do you mean? Did you learn something?"

"I suppose so. I learned today not to get on the wrong side of her."

"Ah, that's a good thing," laughed my mother happily.

Despite my ill-timed reproach, excessively curtailed, the truth is the contents of this strange story impregnated my thoughts over the following days. I wasn't exactly obsessed, but on several occasions the mental images of Attica's adventure helped detract from the boredom of the classroom.

I carried on avoiding Nivardo, but he didn't seem to mind at all. He tried wandering over to me nonchalantly after school, as if nothing was the matter. He registered my contempt from behind his flop of blond hair and gave me back a smile that was as long as a desert. He then gestured with his hand, as if to say, "Women, who can understand them?" or "I've enough problems of my own." The fact is he turned on his heel and ran, like a tame, little dog, back to his pink-lipped princess. How revolting!

This insult gnawed away at me, but I endeavoured to disguise it as best I could. The only person I discussed it with was Muriel, who shared the same desk as me, but I tried to play down its importance.

Muriel, however, knew me better than anybody in the world, and even my evasive look was not enough to throw her off the scent.

"So, you like him, then?" she spat out.

I shook my head, feeling offended, and quickly changed the subject. Her distrustful gaze bored deep inside me, but she didn't insist. Muriel was a good friend.

As far as extra-curricular activities went, my weeks were organized in the following way: Mondays and Wednesdays, I trained with the maila team, while Tuesdays and Thursdays were devoted to my klavia classes in Bagare Street.

So the following Thursday, after school, I traced again the route down to Plugufan. It had started to drizzle, so I ran through the rain, hoping to reach my destination before the mud made my trainers dirty again.

When I got to the old ironmonger's, the notes from the klavia announced my teacher's presence. She wasn't playing a hicupé, but a Gwende composition I was unable to identify. The bell silenced the klavia, leaving only the sound of the wind in the branches of the old oak as a soundtrack to that September sunset.

"Good evening, Guiomar," Mastrina greeted me, holding the door open.

"Good evening, how's it going?"

"Your hair is all wet."

"It's just when I got out of school, it started raining…"

"What's the problem with young people and umbrellas? You prefer to get soaking wet rather than carry one."

"I keep losing them," I confessed, feeling a little ashamed. "I've lost three this year already. I forget them at school, on the bus, in the café… I prefer getting wet than having to put up with Artusa's rebukes."

"Artusa?"

"Our Bru… I mean the Malluma maid who works at home."

Mastrina smiled at me in approval. She went into the kitchen. I observed her movements from the doorway.

"I'm going to make some tea. Would you like some?"

"No, thanks. I'm not a fan of infusions."

"None of them?"

"They're just hot water and herbs. What I find strange is that anyone should like them."

With a mug in her hand, Mastrina led me up the staircase to the klavia room. She sat down slowly in the rocking chair, taking care not to spill her drink. The drops were still sliding down the glass panes of the balcony, but it had stopped raining. The little window in the east was open, and a damp beard hung down from the sill to the floor, where it formed a pool of water on the wood. Through the hole entered the melodious song of some bird.

"Please, Guiomar, would you mind closing the window?"

"It's not raining any more, Mastrina."

"I know. It's not because of the rain, it's because of that preposterous bird."

I closed the window, not understanding the words of my teacher, who seemed to sense the confusion in my expression.

"It's a calandra. It nests in the garden, at the foot of the peach trees."

"Well, it has a very beautiful song."

"The song does not belong to it, it just imitates the trilling of other birds. It sings the whole time. Many nights, it doesn't let me sleep. It does all it can to annoy me."

"A bird?" I asked in surprise.

Mastrina scrunched up her nose.

"Pay no attention. They're just the ravings of an old woman."

I sat down on the stool, hoping to hear more about Attica.

"Right, let's do some scales for ten minutes to warm up those fingers," she ordered.

"Just a moment! We have to start with the story."

"Forget the story. You made it pretty clear on Tuesday that you weren't that interested."

"No way! I was rude, I admit. But I've been thinking about it the last two days. What happened to the girl? Was she captured by the SAN agents?"

Mastrina closed her eyes and leaned against the wicker back of the chair.

"And then you'll do half an hour's scales without complaining?"

"It's a promise!"

I pretended to zip my mouth shut. The shadows of the old tree's branches moved about the room in a phantasmagorical dance of contrasts.

"Now, let's see…"

For almost ten unending minutes, Attica lay motionless on the ground. When the SAN agents finished looking around, they left the ruinous house to continue searching the warren of Bragunde. The attic remained silent until somebody lit an old gas lamp. A twelve-year-old boy stared straight at her.

Attica couldn't take any more. She leaped up, banging her head against a rotten beam. The bearer of the lamp emitted a loud guffaw that echoed around the walls of the shack.

"What are you laughing at, stupid?" said the girl angrily, rubbing her head to lessen the pain.

Old smiley-face came closer. When she saw him, Attica realized it was the boy from the spectacle of the embers, the one who had kept the young people entertained while his accomplices rifled through their wallets. It was the same boy the two SAN agents had held up in the alley.

The girl took off her coat and smacked the cloth with the palm of her hand, trying to get rid of the dust.

"What a mess! These boards have more shit on them than a henhouse!"

"Who would have thought of lying down there?" laughed the boy.

"How was I to know? We were in the dark."

The boy grabbed a twisted stick from the ground and started rubbing Attica's back.

"Let me help you," he said. "If my bug-cleaning stick starts working, there's no stain or daddy-long-legs that can resist!"

"Stop right there!" the girl pushed him away. "Who the hell are you, the little prince from the theatre?"

The ironic tone of the question extinguished the Malluma's smile.

"You think I didn't notice all that nonsense about the child with the iron feet!"

"That's not nonsense. I am a firewalker, as my father was before me."

"Get out of here! I saw those cheap friends of yours poking their fingers into people's pockets," said the Gwende girl.

The boy with the lamp laughed again. He was a little ugly, with a snub nose and a gap between his front teeth.

"You think everything's as easy as it is in your district, don't you?" he countered. "Dumb Chiona! We weren't stealing anything, we were just encouraging people's sense of solidarity. In times like these, you have to give people a helping hand if you want to get paid for your work."

"You call that 'work'? You didn't even do anything. Apart from playing the fool, of course."

"I didn't have enough time."

Attica put her coat on again with a disbelieving look painted on her face.

"Don't you worry," insisted the boy, "one day I'll show you what I'm capable of."

One after the other, they climbed down the rope and left their hiding place. The card games were already over, and the alley was deserted. The plague of scorpions seemed to be growing, and the people of Bragunde had filled up the gaps beneath their doors with cloths and towels to protect their homes from the waves of insects passing through the nabrallo.

They circled around the shack and walked silently along the street, retracing the route Attica had taken in her flight earlier.

"Do you know what time it is?" asked the girl. "I lost my watch in all that scuffle."

"Hello, my name's Fuco. Pleased to meet you! You're welcome, don't mention it. Saving confused little Chionas from being trapped by brutes is just a hobby."

Attica puffed up her cheeks and glanced at Fuco, who was brashly jumping on top of the lines of scorpions.

"You saved me?"

"Do you have a problem with that?"

"You're forgetting you're the one who was whimpering in the alley."

"Rubbish. I had it all under control."

"What, like this?"

The girl imitated the crying of a baby, rubbing her eyes with her forefingers.

The little boy stuffed his hands in his pockets and pursed his lips, feeling offended. Attica, who soon felt sorry for making fun of him, decided to change the subject.

"You didn't tell me what time it was."

Fuco stopped walking and placed the palms of his hands on either side of his mouth, creating a megaphone.

"What time is it???" he belted out.

"Quarter past eleven!!!" came the reply from inside one of the houses on the street.

Attica opened her eyes wide in a mixture of amusement and amazement.

"See?" laughed Fuco. "A Malluma is never without a watch."

The girl suddenly realized she had a serious problem.

"Oh shit, shit and double shit!" she moaned.

"What is it?"

"Quarter past eleven! The last train back to Plugufan was at ten past."

"Well, there's not much you can do about that," remarked

48

Fuco. "Was somebody going to wait for you?"

"My brother, though he'll probably think I've gone to sleep at a friend's house."

"You just live with your brother?"

"And my mother as well... though she hardly sets foot in the house."

"Well, don't worry. You can always stay with me. I'm just going to see Onga to ask her where all these damn insects are coming from."

"Onga?"

"Onga the Great, the Queen of the Cemetery! Have you never heard of her?"

"Never."

"Well, that's a surprise," said the boy. "Kilometres of distance and centuries of ignorance – the tragedy of our two races."

Fuco came over to Attica and whispered in her ear.

"Onga's a witch, a soothsayer. She's supposed to be more than a hundred and fifty years old," the boy glanced theatrically to both sides, to make sure no one was listening to their conversation. "They say the secret of her old age comes from eating the hearts of freshly-buried corpses."

"Ugh, that's disgusting!" exclaimed Attica.

"Disgusting or not, that's a fact."

The squared maze of Bragunde was nodding off beneath the poor street lighting. On its walls could be read a whole host of proclamations on different themes. Some expressed amorous sentiments, such as "I love you, Antigone" or "Baruc and Anaïs." Others expressed support for the local pilco team, a sport that was hugely popular in the nabrallos. And then there were those of a more political nature, demanding freedom and rights for the Malluma people.

Once far away from the main avenue, which criss-crossed the nabrallo, running parallel to the railway, it was difficult to distinguish one street from another. They were made up of long lines of Siamese houses crammed full of inhabitants, owing to the uncontrolled increase in the population. Some of the houses were built of brick and asbestos roofs, but most were just sheds made of planks, cardboard and other refuse. Those privileged windows that had glass in them reflected the light of the full moon, which modestly concealed its belly behind scraps of white gauze.

"Tell me," asked Fuco, "had you been to Bragunde before?"

"This is my first time."

"Is it as you imagined?"

"No, to be frank. Perhaps the bit in the centre, next to the station, is. But all this... North of the loke, not much is said about the nabrallos. They're just something down there, at the end of the railway, almost in another world."

"It's not easy round here. As the old people say, 'No solid roof, no pot of hot food, no mother to remove your nits.'"

They headed down a street that descended slowly towards a sea of darkness. The slope was paved with small, grey stones, many of which had come up, leaving a whole rash of cubic holes along the way. As they approached the end of the street, an open field appeared in front of them that was bordered by a high, white wall. As the houses finished, so did the paving, and the two walkers entered an expanse of flattened grass. Fuco informed Attica there was a market there during the day.

"Come on!" insisted the boy, going faster so he could reach the iron gate that protected the entrance first. He grabbed the bars with both hands and looked at Attica. "This is Bragunde Cemetery."

The girl peered through the railings and saw a gloomy landscape of tombstones dotted here and there. The marble of the tombs shone in the moonlight, and a strangely warm breeze whistled through the cypress leaves.

"Do we really have to go in there?"

"You can do what you like, I'm going to find Onga!"

"But why?"

"Because of the scorpions, I told you."

Attica scratched her head, unwilling to enter the cemetery.

"I know about that, but why do you have to go? Wouldn't it be better for an adult to go looking for Onga?"

"Adult or child, everybody in Bragunde is afraid of Onga."

"And aren't you?"

"I'm from Zambela."

A heavy chain joined the two sections of the gate, so to get inside the enclosure you had to clamber up the railings. Fuco was the first to undertake the climb. Attica copied him a little later, placing her thick-soled boots between the bars of the other section. Once up, they hung down the other side of the gate and dropped to the ground. The cemetery smelled of earth and freshly-mown grass.

If the streets in Bragunde formed a perfect grid, the cemetery was completely the opposite: a chaotic arrangement of tombstones and fancy mausoleums stretching across an endless plain. There was no fixed path, so they had to pick their way among the tombstones.

Fuco led the way determinedly, but after a while he stopped to look hesitantly around. Attica sat down on a tombstone and watched the boy, whose face had adopted a worried expression. In the sky, clouds played with the clarity of the moonlight, casting grotesque shadows on the marble.

"Now what?" asked the girl.

"Let me think," pleaded Fuco. Attica realized he was petrified. "I've never been here at night. We have to find the little chapel. Underneath is the crypt where Onga lives... so they say. I reckon it's that way."

They started walking in the direction the boy had indicated, though Attica suspected he'd chosen this route at random.

Suddenly a large, thick cloud hid the moon, plunging them into darkness. The screech of a barn owl resounded above their heads. Fuco clung to the girl.

"A barn owl, the bird of night," he whimpered, his vocal cords twanging loosely. "It's not a good sign."

Attica brushed him away with her arm.

"Let's keep going," she insisted.

They felt their way forwards, taking care not to trip on a stone and go crashing to the ground. Even so, Attica banged her shin on an iron grate that surrounded a tomb. She bit her lower lip to smother a yelp of pain.

"This is madness," admitted Fuco. "We can't go on like this, we can't see a thing. It's better to go back."

"So that's the courage of a Zambelan," mocked the girl.

"I'm just being practical, my dear Chiona. There's no point in cracking our heads open."

Attica came to a halt and listened out for the sound of the boy's breathing.

"OK then," she said to the dark. "Let's go back."

"Hang on to my jersey," suggested Fuco.

Feeling their way, they endeavoured to retrace the route they had taken, inching forwards with tiny steps.

At some point, Fuco stepped on nothing and fell into a hole, pulling Attica down with him. As their bodies hit the bottom of the ditch, a cloud of dust arose, which made them cough.

"You clumsy fool!" complained the girl, rubbing her bruised back. "Look what you've gone and done!"

"I swear this hole wasn't here on the way. I think I've hurt my foot."

The two children plumped down on the earth. In the sky, the cloud finally released the moon, and the atmosphere was again illuminated by its electric gleam. They were inside an open, empty grave. They looked upwards. The edge of the hole was a couple of yards above them. Between the two of them, it shouldn't be too difficult to escape their captivity.

But they hadn't reckoned on a further difficulty: a heavy tombstone slowly creaked over the edge, swallowing up the clarity of night. A little later, a Malluma boy and a Gwende girl had been buried alive in Bragunde Cemetery■

"And that's the end of the story for today," announced Mastrina, getting up from the rocking chair with an empty mug in her hand.

"Oh no, not again!" I complained bitterly. "You can't keep on stopping like that."

"Remember our deal, Guiomar. You still haven't learned anything about the klavia."

"But I've learned lots about life, haven't I?" I laughed while reaching out to stroke one of the cats, who backed away across the carpet in distrust.

"Well, I suppose so," replied Mastrina. "One never stops learning about life."

BLEOXANOL-BR is a dual-action medicine that combines the effects of an antibiotic (slowing down the growth of damaging cells) with those of a painkiller (bringing moderate to severe pain under control).

It is used mainly for combating Volbloede or ancestral blood complaint, which some Gwende women contract after a miscarriage.

BLEOXANOL-BR

ⓘ

BEFORE YOU U

Nowadays, it's almost impossible not to bump into a bunch of foreigners wherever you go in Plugufan, but a couple of decades ago, when I was a teenager, this was far less common. The few visitors that came to Audierna back then, almost always because of work, would stay in Seina, the financial district in the east of the city. The most you could expect was for a couple of pedestrians to head down in the evening, after a day's work, to the bank of the River Ioke, from where they would observe with interest the jumble of cranes helping to build new Gwende colonies in the south.

Now Plugufan has turned into an amusement park for people in search of Audierna's pure essence, and flocks of tourists equipped with cameras mill about its streets. Every couple of yards, an itinerant musician plays his instrument and, at the stalls in Decature Street market, prints, flowers, old coins and hundreds of other trinkets are on display. Sellers secretly offering bottles of likeur and young boys handing out restaurant flyers complete the modern landscape in this old quarter. And yet years ago, this zone was the physical symbol of a despicable historical injustice, although the centre of political decision-making had already moved west to the district of Linne some time earlier.

Had any one of those businessmen wandered down the streets of Plugufan in the week when my story resumes, he would undoubtedly have got very wet. It was pouring down, and the old quarter had taken on a sad, even ridiculous appearance, having been designed to imitate towns in the north and not to endure such austral winters. The streets were all muddy, the walls besmirched, and the roofs, tired and weak, could hardly complete their mission of keeping homes dry.

The rosebushes on the avenue that ran parallel to the river were bare, frozen and shrivelled, their leaves weeping tears of greyish water that was reminiscent of molten lead.

It had rained on Saturday and Sunday. Monday had seen a temporary truce, which the sky broke on Tuesday with unexpected fury. That was my day for studying the klavia, so after school I ran like a madwoman in the direction of Bagare Street. Heeding Mastrina's advice, that morning I had left home with an umbrella in my hand. But a sudden gust of wind had broken its ribs on my first attempt to use it. Feeling annoyed and cursing my luck, I'd ended up throwing it in the bin.

When I rang at the door of my teacher's house, I was soaked to the skin. The kitchen light was on, revealing her presence on the ground floor, so it didn't take her long to open. The cat with the spot on its nose came with her, but sheltered behind the old woman's body from the powerful downpour that was hammering the roof of the porch.

"Guiomar, please!" exclaimed the old woman on seeing me so wet.

"I swear I had an umbrella."

"Come with me."

I followed her to the bathroom, where she rummaged about in a drawer and pulled out two towels, one large and one small. They were both mint-green with red flowers along the edges.

"Take these," she said, handing them to me. "Get undressed and dry yourself properly. I'll bring you some clean clothes."

She left the bathroom and disappeared down the corridor towards that part of the house I hadn't been to yet. I pushed the door to and started taking off my clothes. Coat, cardigan, blouse, skirt, tights... all soaked. I looked at myself in the cabinet mirror. My hair was plastered to my shoulders, and my nose was red from the cold. The cat with the spot pushed the door open a little and poked its head into the bathroom, staring at me. What had happened to its companions? They were probably fast asleep on the balcony. In fact, I didn't recall ever having seen them downstairs.

I was trembling like a leaf. The bathroom smelled of bleach and air freshener. The decoration was shabby and old-fashioned. Behind a curtain marked with black damp spots, the bathtub in one of the corners boasted a plastic orchid. Some embroidered cloths covered the loo-roll dispenser and the cistern. I opened the door of the cabinet. A whole host of jars of medication like the one I had seen Mastrina take out of her pocket on my first visit were perfectly lined up. On labels stuck to the bellies of these containers was written the name of a medicine: BLEOXANOL-BR.

Some footsteps could be heard in the corridor, so I quickly closed the cabinet door.

"Let's see if this will do," remarked Mastrina. "Give me your wet clothes, I'll put them to dry next to the heater."

I exchanged my bundle of wet clothes for some nicely-folded garments that smelled of camphor. She must have noticed my embarrassment at appearing like this, all cold and in my underclothes, because she closed the door to the bathroom.

I put on the garments she had given me. First, a flannel skirt with large yellow and brown squares, which hung from the top of my waist to a good span below my knees. I then put on a white blouse that was a little tight for me and a thick, overstretched cardigan. To round off my unusual outfit, I wrapped the small towel around my head in the form of a turban. Looking at myself in the mirror again, I wondered what Muriel and the other girls would say if they could see me like this.

As I was climbing the stairs, a happy melody came from the klavia, silencing the drumming of the rain on the roof. Mastrina smiled when she saw me. She seemed in a good mood, and her white hair shone in the pale light of the lamp on the ceiling. A flash of lightning momentarily lit up the room, like a camera flash. This was followed by a loud rumble of thunder that frightened the cats on the balcony and sent them scurrying beneath the klavia.

"See? They also like hicupé," said Mastrina in amusement. "Sit down next to me."

I grabbed a stool that was leaning against the shelves and sat down next to the enthusiastic player. Her fingers, long and arthritic, jumped over the keys at an astonishing speed.

"C-E-F-F-C, C-E-F-F-C…" she hummed.

I started playing the accompaniment. Shyly and a little sluggishly to begin with, but I soon got the hang of it and even ended up improvising a little.

"Very good!" the teacher encouraged me.

I was playing duets with Mastrina Xaoven! I wished my mother could see me. The piece got faster and faster until my fingers were no longer able to keep up with the frenetic pace set by the old lady. So I abruptly stopped playing and started clapping in time to the music. Mastrina gave a final flourish, sweeping her hands up and down the keys. Both of us burst out laughing and frightened the cats again.

"Very good, very good," she congratulated me a little breathlessly, "that was a fine duet."

"You really think so!"

"Of course! We'd be a real sensation in the clubs of Zambela."

"What about those in Bragunde?"

"Well, that's another story entirely. They're very demanding there, you know."

I got up from the stool and plumped my bottom on the carpet, crossing my legs. Mastrina stared at my bare feet.

"Would you like some socks?"

"No, thanks, I'm fine. It's quite warm in here."

The cat with the pink spot came over and rubbed up against my legs. I stroked its head, and it immediately started purring.

"The cat with the pink nose is the only one I recognize," I said.

"Well, they may not look it, but they're actually very different. This one's the most affectionate, the one on the right is the bravest, and that one… That's the greediest of the lot."

I spent a few seconds gazing at the other two felines, which were absent-mindedly licking their bodies beneath the instrument.

"Since I did so well, why don't we carry on with Attica's story?" I ventured unconvincingly. And yet my words had the desired effect. Mastrina smiled indulgently and got up from her stool.

"Let me just sit down in my usual place."

J ust as the tombstone stopped creaking, causing Fuco and Attica's blood to freeze, there could be heard a distant voice that asked:

"Who are you and what are you doing here, what are you doing?"

The voice had a strange, rough and deep solemnity, drawing out the "t"s in the usual Malluma way. Attica felt her heart beating furiously inside her chest. Her throat was dry and her eyes were watery because of the dust in the ditch. She was wondering what to do when, emerging from the darkness, she heard her companion's shout:

"My name is Barucus Fuco, son of Dantus Baruc the Firewalker!"

Nobody answered. In the darkness, all that could be heard was the children's rapid breathing. The boy decided to insist.

"My name is Barucus Fuco, son of..."

"Yes, I heard you the first time, dumbo, I heard you," the voice interrupted him. "You still haven't said what it is you're doing here and who the Chiona with you is."

Attica felt for Fuco with her fingers. When she found him, she grabbed him by the neck of his jersey.

"Tell her to get us out of here," she hissed.

Her back was drenched in sweat, and her head was pounding, as if it was about to burst.

"Do you think she's going to listen to me?" Fuco defended himself, also in a whisper.

The girl collapsed against one of the earthen walls. Fear had paralyzed her legs, and a terrible pain had taken hold of every fibre in her body, preventing her from breathing freely. She didn't like enclosed spaces.

As a little girl, one night in August, Attica had been travelling with her brother in the back seat of a car. They were returning home after a party, and her mother was driving. She had drunk a lot and didn't stop crying and cursing somebody all the way. In a poorly-managed manoeuvre, she lost control of the vehicle, which ended up falling into the River Ioke. They slowly sank into the turbid waters, amid shouts of terror. They were rescued by some students coming home after a night on the town. "A miracle," according to the local press. The girl attributed the uncontrollable fear she felt in dark, enclosed spaces to this experience.

"We have come to consult Onga the Great!" affirmed Fuco. "The Chiona with me is a powerful witch!"

"A witch?" protested Attica in a whisper. "What made you say such a stupid thing?"

"What do you expect?" replied the boy. "There's no way of thinking straight in this hole."

Incredibly, Fuco's strategy worked, and the gigantic tombstone started creaking again above their heads, allowing the moonlight to flood in. A man's enormous, bald head peered into the hole, gazing at them with curiosity.

"Please, help us out of here," pleaded Fuco.

The man remained motionless, not even blinking, and showed no signs of lending them a hand. Then another silhouette appeared above the ditch. It was a very old woman with a swarthy face. She was wearing a peculiar rabbit-skin cap and was wrapped in a black, threadbare cloak. She can't have been more than five feet tall, but her bottomless gaze afforded her a powerful presence. She was leaning on a thick stick that was taller than she was and crowned by a handful of feathers from different birds. The woman stared at them for a couple of seconds before gesturing to the bald man to help them. The man bent over the edge of the grave and stretched out his hand.

Fuco grabbed the huge hand and was pulled up. After that, it was Attica's turn, and she repeated the operation.

"Thanks," said the girl to the giant.

"He can't hear you, he can't. He's deaf," the woman informed her.

Attica scrutinized the old woman's face, which was smooth and dark, with two bags hanging under her small, black eyes. An archipelago of chestnut-brown marks spread across her large, plump cheeks, in the midst of which sprouted a little snub nose. Her long, woody neck, like the branch of an old tree, was surrounded by dozens of leather necklaces with shiny beads that jangled noisily whenever the old woman moved.

"Are you Onga?" inquired Fuco.

"I am."

"Well, that's great! We wanted to ask..."

"Stop right there! I'm the one who asks questions round here. First of all, how dare you enter one of our sacred places in the company of a Chiona, how dare you?"

"She's a witch."

The old woman banged the little boy's head with the stick, and he let out a yelp of pain.

"A witch, says the impostor!" exclaimed Onga.

Fuco, realizing the game was up, pleaded to Attica for help; the girl simply lowered her gaze, not knowing what to do.

"It isn't good for us to be here, it isn't good," said Onga. "Follow us to the crypt, follow us."

The old woman took the giant's hand and walked alongside him, leaning on her stick. Fuco and Attica followed behind them. From time to time, the clouds would settle on the moon, plunging them back into darkness and forcing the children to orient themselves by the sound of the witch's stick banging on the ground.

"It isn't far, it isn't."

They reached a small, square, marble temple, the steps of which were guarded by the trunk of a dried peach tree. The building could easily have been mistaken for one of the large mausoleums, had it not been for the liturgical symbols engraved along the frieze, which rested on five sturdy columns.

Onga and the giant climbed the steps and entered the temple. The children went after them carefully. The inside of the building was lit by two torches on opposite walls. The bald man took one of them and went down a narrow, stone staircase hidden in one of the corners. The others followed him to the basement, a low-ceilinged crypt brimming with curious artefacts: the walls were lined with shelves full of jars with the bodies of snakes and mice immersed in a greenish liquid; in the middle of the room was a long, crude table covered in bottles, handfuls of herbs and strange, metal instruments; there were also some large, copper cauldrons with fire-blackened bellies; pushed up against the walls, several boxes contained piles of old books, their leather covers hidden beneath a thick layer of dust; from the ceiling hung three cages, each with a bird in, although the only bird Attica recognized was an enigmatic and beautiful magpie that fixed its jet-black eyes on the visitors.

The giant withdrew to a corner and sat on a stool, leaning back against the rough, stone wall. He then closed his eyes and disconnected from the world.

Onga went over to the table and rummaged among the things until she found a large, golden bowl.

"Come on then, tell me: what is it you're after, what is it?"

Fuco coughed to clear his throat and, bowing reverentially, addressed the witch:

"O powerful Onga, Queen of the Cemetery, Lady of Death..."

"Stop with the nonsense and get on with it, get on with it!"

"Well, this Chiona girl and I, risking your more than justified rage, but appealing to your renowned sense of indulgence, have dared to enter your dominions in order to consult you, O Mother of the Night. We may be a pair of sad fools, but we are also good people and fearful citizens. We are worried, Lady of the Darkness, about this strange plague that overwhelms Bragunde, all those scorpions that disturb your people's peace of mind with their long lines."

Onga listened to the boy's words without flinching. She then placed her hands on the table and leaned forwards, remaining in this posture for a good while, deep in thought. Attica and Fuco glanced at each other, wondering what to do. This place gave the girl the willies. Had she obeyed the impulses of her body, she would have greased her shins and got the hell out of that scabby hole, though the idea of wandering around the enormous cemetery all on her own didn't exactly appeal to her either.

"You, Chiona, give me your hand, give me," said Onga finally.

Attica took a step towards the table and shakily held out the palm of her left hand.

"The appearance of the pilgrims is an old sign, the appearance," hissed the witch, holding the girl's hand firmly.

Onga's fingers resembled ornate sticks that ended in long, grimy, twisted nails.

"Are you afraid, Chiona?"

"Um... no," said Attica rather unconvincingly.

"That's right..." laughed the old woman, revealing a paltry set of teeth from which several pieces were missing.

With surprising speed, Onga grabbed a knife from the table and ran its blade over the girl's palm, creating a wound that soon began to bleed profusely. The girl cried out in pain and tried unsuccessfully to get her arm back, which was being held firmly by the wrist.

"Calm down," Onga reassured her, "the worst is over, the worst."

Attica felt dizzy. Tears formed two lenses in her eyes, which provided a deformed view of the crypt. The old witch grabbed a large bowl and placed it under the wound, gathering the drops of blood that soon formed a red pool.

Fuco observed the scene in silence, biting hard on his lower lip.

"Let's see if you're who I think you are, let's see," mused Onga. "We will soon find out, we will."

Fuco pulled a crumpled handkerchief out of his pocket, which he offered the girl so she could bandage her wound. In the meantime, Onga bent down to the ground to grab a handful of earth, which she threw inside the bowl. She then spat on the mixture and stirred it with the nail of her little finger, emitting a foul screech that aroused the giant on his stool.

"I dreamed of you, I dreamed," declared Onga, gazing at the revolting mass. "The problem is beneath our feet, the problem. It is in the Great Cave."

"The Great Cave?" said Fuco in astonishment, opening his eyes wide. "Do you mean...?"

"Nigrofe, the Great Cave, the Green Country, the Hearth of the Monastery... It has had dozens of names throughout its history, it has. That is where you'll find your answers, you must enter the earth."

Fuco shivered and cleared his throat.

"O powerful Onga, Sister of the Little Owl, how can we poor wretches enter the earth?"

"What ways do you know of entering the earth? The earth is entered by dead people and moles. It won't help very much if you enter the earth being dead, so try to find a mole to follow, try."

"A mole?"

"Yes, a mole. There are moles that devote themselves only to digging tunnels. But then there are moles that like feeling the sun on their faces and watch over the tunnels dug by others. That is the mole you have to find, that is. If you're the ones the blood talks about, if you're the ones the earth cries out for, if you're the ones the water exalts, then it won't be difficult for you to find it. If not, then stop wasting my time, stop."

"This is ridiculous..." protested Attica with pursed lips.

"You're the one who's ridiculous, ignorant Chiona!" thundered Onga with a powerful voice. "As are ridiculous the auguries that point to you. But who am I, silly old woman, to dispute the choices of the Spirit of Dendria, who am I? All those insects are just a silly joke compared with the evil lurking beneath us. Now beat it! There is still lots to do, there is still."

The two children legged it out of the crypt. In the sky, the moon continued jumping around with the ethereal, nocturnal gauzes, and a warm breeze shook the branches of the trees. Occasionally bumping into tombstones, grates and bushes, the pair felt their way back to the high wall that surrounded the enclosure. There, they followed the white surface back to the iron gate, which they climbed over again to reach the open field.

"Cripes!" exclaimed Fuco a little breathlessly. "My legs are still trembling. That woman's off her head! Pilgrims, moles, auguries... what on earth was she talking about?"

The boy collapsed on the flattened grass, felt in his pocket and pulled out a small packet of tobacco. Then, still trembling, he rolled a wonky cigarette, put it in his mouth and lit it.

Attica, who had remained standing out of fear of the scorpions, grabbed the cigarette, took a drag and stamped it out on the grass, which was coated in frost.

"How old are you, dwarf?"

"Sixteen."

"Down a bit!"

"Fourteen."

"Keep going..."

"OK then, I'm twelve. But twelve in a nabrallo is the same as twenty-four north of the loke, just so you know. I'm a mature type."

"I can see that!"

The two children gazed at Bragunde, immense and hopeless, sleeping spectrally in the moonlight. A strange, monotonous hum hung in the night air.

Having recovered their energy, they headed towards the houses. They climbed the deserted slope in silence, occasionally kicking the loose stones on the pavement. It was early morning, and the steam from their mouths revealed how cold it was at that hour.

As the slope levelled out, they turned right, entering a maze of alleyways. To Attica, each street they went down looked just like the one before, a succession of low shacks lined up alongside a river of mud. The pair's shadows danced all over the walls. On the ground, the lines of scorpions had abandoned the haste of evening and sunk into an expectant state of lethargy.

In the distance could be heard the hullabaloo of a party. They slowly drew closer. It was coming from one of the tunnels that joined the two halves of Bragunde, which the railway dissected. The sounds of a malgrine and a litenklave playing a lively hicupé merged with enthusiastic whoops and clapping.

The skeletons of old cars were piled up in the open area that preceded the tunnel. On the ground, several puddles reflected a distorted moon that was stained by the iridescent colours of petrol on the water.

"Cover your head," Fuco asked Attica.

The girl put on her hood. In the tunnel, she couldn't repress the enormous smile that filled her face. How many Gwendes could honestly say they'd been to a real Malluma party? Probably very few, and now Attica was one of them. She relished the look there would be on Olaf's face when she told him the following Monday.

"Fuco! Hey, Fuco!" shouted a group of children, who were squatting down and playing dice against the wall. "Won't you join us?"

"Not today, my friends," replied the boy, waving to them.

This negative acted like a spring that brought several members of the group to their feet. Shouting and cajoling, they did their best to get the boy to join them.

"Come on, just a quick game!" suggested one.

"You can't say no!" insisted another. "You cleared me out yesterday. You owe me a rematch."

Fuco gazed at Attica, turning his back on the pleading children.

"I'm going to have a word with this lot. Wait here a moment, I won't be long."

The boy ran off. Attica looked around. The tunnel was full of dozens of people. Some of them, like Fuco's friends, were noisily playing dice or cards; others had formed couples next to the musicians and were twisting and turning to the music, as Attica had seen them do in the club the previous evening. From several metal drums emerged red beards of fire, scattering sparks that flew up and were then extinguished against the vaulted ceiling.

"Lady, won't you give me a crust of bread?" asked a toothless, scraggy man. Until he spoke, Attica had failed to notice his presence.

"I don't have any," answered the girl, disguising her Gwende accent as best she could.

"Please, lady, I'm hungry. Just a little crust."

"Really, I don't have any."

Attica began to feel bothered by the man's insistence. She could smell his repulsive breath inching closer. She was just wondering whether to go in search of Fuco when she felt the pointed end of a knife pressing against her stomach.

"Do something stupid, and I'll turn you into mincemeat," warned the man. "Walk in front of me."

Forced by the dagger, the girl headed towards the exit of the tunnel. Fuco was joking and laughing with the children with the dice. He glanced at where Attica should have been and was surprised by her absence. He moved away from the group to get a better look of the open area in front of the tunnel. He saw the girl walking off in the distance, near the exit that led to the western part of the nabrallo. A man was following close behind her, practically pushing her along.

Fuco ran after them. Outside the tunnel, he was just about to catch them up when two giants grabbed him under the arms and lifted him into the air. Despite his protests, the boy was powerless to prevent himself being thrown into the boot of one of the abandoned vehicles. The noise from the party was so strong it drowned out his shouts. Once the boot was closed, he tried to kick it open, but was unable. Realizing the difficulty he was in, he settled down in his prison as best he could and prepared to wait■

Sime Cake Shop

DAILY ELABORATION OF FINE PASTRIES

IN THIS FAMILY BUSINESS, YOU WILL FIND THE BEST CISTÉS IN ALL AUDIERNA, BAKED IN THE TRADITIONAL STYLE AND WITH ALL THE LOVE AND CARE WITH WHICH TOBALDO SIME FOUNDED THIS HOUSE MORE THAN A CENTURY AGO.

32 Decature Street. Plugufan

The following Thursday, I found Mastrina's house immersed in silence and full of shadows. She greeted me briefly when she opened the door and, without saying anything else, went upstairs, dragging her feet. With her last drops of energy, she reached the rocking chair and lowered her shrivelled body into it.

"Please, Guiomar, switch on the light and sit down at the klavia."

Seeing she wasn't in the mood, I obeyed her silently. I spent almost two hours mercilessly destroying a very simple composition by Mastrino Tangue. Old Xaoven corrected every one of my mistakes from the chair, first wagging her forefinger and then gesturing to me to go back to the beginning of the line.

And so the clock ticked slowly down until it was time for the end of the class.

"That's enough for today," declared Mastrina, rescuing me from this torture.

I got up from the stool, visibly annoyed. For goodness' sake! Attica's story was the only reason for my continued visits to Bagare Street. I was dying to find out how this new danger threatening her would pan out. Who cared about Tangue's ridiculous music?

Mastrina quickly sensed my disappointment. As I passed next to the rocking chair, she grabbed my wrist. I gazed into her glassy, sunken eyes. She looked like a bird that has been in a hailstorm.

"I'm not feeling too well today," she said.

"I know," I replied, essaying a smile, "is there something I can do for you?"

"You can make more of an effort with the klavia."

She endeavoured to return my smile, though all she managed was a grimace of pain. She breathed in deeply and spoke again.

"What I like best on Saturdays in autumn is baking a good cisté and tucking into it with some nice hot chocolate."

"I love cisté, especially the one my father makes," I admitted.

"Well, without wishing to detract from Mr Brelivete's cisté, you should try mine. Though I suppose a girl of your age has lots of other things to do on a Saturday afternoon…"

"Not at all!" I interrupted her excitedly. "My social life's a disaster!"

This made her really smile, as if my sudden enthusiasm had acted as a balm for her aches and pains.

"In which case, why don't you come round, and we can attend to unfinished business?" she winked at me.

"What time should I come?"

"About five would be best."

I squeezed her hand in a gesture of intimacy that was unusual for me.

"See you at five then," I agreed before heading down the stairs towards the exit.

It was cold the following Saturday, though a luminous sun helped the city shake off the night's frost. A thick mist, like cotton, rose slowly in the south, beyond the territory of Plugufan, from the crack drawn by the River Ioke across Audierna.

That morning, I helped my mother fold about a million sheets and towels. We placed them in the drawers of the dresser, crowning them with sprigs of lavender to give them a nice smell. This task could easily have been performed by Artusa during the week, but my mother was a bit of an obsessive when it came to sheets and towels. She seemed to actually enjoy buying, washing and ironing them. Everybody has their oddities.

At lunchtime, we sat down in the living room, where my father ceremoniously served up an enormous, smoking bowl of gwebraae. The old man lunched outside from Monday to Friday – he worked in an office in Seina, about an hour away by train from our district, Fundete, so at weekends he was dying to show off his culinary skills, which were more imaginary than real. It was impossible on a Saturday to escape estokuise with salty potato purée or a gwebraae like this one, which, while not amazing, was at least edible.

After lunch, as my family rested for a while, I got on with my homework. At four fifteen, I left what I was doing, put on my coat and headed for the door, preparing to walk to Plugufan.

"Where are you going?" asked my mother, lying on the sofa with one eye still closed. She was probably hoping to continue with the business of the sheets until dinnertime.

"Mastrina's house."

"What for?"

I decided to answer with a half-truth to avoid having to go into detail.

"The other day, she wasn't feeling too well. I want to see how she is."

"Well, look at that!" exclaimed my mother. "I hope she feels better soon."

"I'll send her your best wishes," I promised, giving my mother a peck on the cheek in farewell.

On Saturday afternoons, Bagare Street was heaving. At weekends, Plugufan filled with people from all over Audierna who came in their droves to visit their elderly relatives. If the weather was pleasant as well, the result was pavements crammed with pedestrians that huddled in little groups.

The house had yet to show its face from behind the old ironmonger's when the scent of hot chocolate hit my nose. For no particular reason, I ran the last few yards. I could see my teacher's silhouette busying about the kitchen, behind the lace curtain. I pressed the bell and waited. As she opened the front door, the three ginger cats used this opportunity to scamper off down the street as if they were being harried by the devil.

"Hey, where do you think you're going so fast?" I shouted as they slipped among the bushes of one of the vacant lots in the street.

"Don't worry," Mastrina reassured me. "They've gone to stretch their legs. They won't be long."

I found the old woman in a state that veered between happiness and fatigue. She seemed to have used up a lot of her energy getting tea ready. She sat on a chair in the kitchen and pointed to the cisté, which glistened cheerfully on the table. Meanwhile, the hot chocolate simmered merrily on the stove.

"What do you think?" she said proudly. "Not even the President eats it as fresh as that."

"It looks wonderful," I replied sincerely, "but if you want an informed opinion, I'll have to try a piece."

Mastrina placed her hands on the table and tried to stand up. After two unsuccessful attempts, I held her under the arms and helped her to her feet.

"Thanks, Guiomar," she whispered, a little embarrassed. "I was thinking we could have tea upstairs. The sun comes in from the balcony at this time, and it's very pleasant."

"Let me help you."

I put my arm around her waist. She hardly weighed anything at all. She was like one of those straw-filled scarecrows they burn in towns of the north in June. I left her upstairs, sitting in her rocking chair, and went back down to the kitchen to fetch the tea.

"Turn off the stove, will you?" she cried down the stairs. "And be careful not to burn yourself!"

I wish she'd spoken sooner. As I reached out to remove the pot from the stove, I felt a sharp pain in my middle finger. I immediately placed it under the tap and turned on the cold water, which was enough to ease the pain, but not to prevent a blister rising on my finger. I grabbed a tablecloth from one of the kitchen cupboards and placed it under my arm, freeing my hands so I could grab the pot by the handles and carry it upstairs. I placed the hot chocolate on the round table and went back in search of the cisté. Once all the tea was in the klavia room, I filled one mug with hot chocolate and offered it to Mastrina. I then cut a piece of cake, left it where she could reach it, and served myself a generous portion.

"Mastrina Xaoven, do you have any other pupils?" I asked.

The old woman rocked in her chair with a smile.

"You know my health isn't great. I don't think I could cope with another one like you."

I then did something really stupid: I sat on the round stool and, without thinking, placed the mug of hot chocolate on the lid of the klavia. Mastrina let out a howl as if she'd just been branded with a hot iron on her buttocks.

"Are you out of your mind???"

It took me a few seconds to realize what the problem was. Fortunately, my negligence didn't leave a mark on the white lacquer, otherwise I would have had to jump off the balcony in order to save my skin.

I decided to hold the mug in my hands and sat down on the carpet, crossing my legs. The cisté was succulent, and I said this to the cook, who responded with a happy smile.

"You'd like to know what happened to Attica, wouldn't you?" she asked.

"Well, I didn't want to be rude," I answered with my mouth full, "but I was wondering when you'd get down to business!"

Attica walked very stiffly, feeling the point of the knife pressing into her back.

"Turn right," ordered the man.

They entered a narrow street flanked by brick walls that were unusually high for a nabrallo. The place was dark, silent, and stank of rotten food. Attica perceived a hidden presence in the half-shadows. A line of scorpions ran over the ground with its usual mechanical movement.

"So?" came a voice in the darkness.

"So what?" replied the man with the dagger angrily. "Hand it over, I haven't got all night."

A shadow approached the girl and covered her head with a sack that reeked of petrol. The pressure of the knife on her back was removed.

"As we agreed," said the new voice as a few coins were exchanged. Then, without further ado, some footsteps retreated.

"Now you're coming with me," said her new kidnapper. "Behave yourself!"

Unlike the man with the knife, this one spoke in a pleasant, almost paternal whisper. That did not suffice, however, to calm the girl's nerves. A hand grabbed hold of her arm and forced her to start walking.

They snaked their way through the alleys of Bragunde in complete silence. When they came to a halt, her companion knocked on a wooden door. A moment later, some rusty hinges disturbed the nabrallo's silent night with their groan.

"In you go, little missy," whispered the man in her ear. "Careful, there are two steps down."

Inside the room, Attica could hear the murmur of several low voices.

"Take off the mask," ordered the voice of a boy.

Somebody pulled off the sack, and the murmur of voices immediately ceased. In front of her was a small, grotty tavern lit only by three candles that were just about to go out on top of three rough, little tables.

It was, thought Attica, the typical kind of place her mother would not set foot in even if she was being pursued by a herd of buffalo. Sitting at one of the tables, an old man tucked into an enormous jug of stout. Next to the bar, a short man smoked his pipe while another, strong and wearing a leather waistcoat, cracked his knuckles. Behind the bar, the waitress fixed Attica with a nasty look. She must have been about forty, her dark hair tied in a ponytail that fell down the valley formed by her abundant cleavage. The only one who didn't seem to have noticed the girl's presence was a bald old man with a wooden leg, who was chasing a scorpion that had managed to enter the bar with a broom.

One by one, the looks of those present were directed away from Attica towards a dark corner, where somebody was chewing away to their heart's content.

"Do you know who I am?" asked the boy who had given the order to uncover her head from the half-shadows.

"Somebody who speaks with their mouth full," replied Attica challengingly.

The boy stopped eating and dropped the metal plate he was holding on the table, making a loud clanging noise.

"Do you know who I am?" he repeated more seriously.

"Why, should I?"

"Oh yes, you should."

"The President of the Confederation?"

The boy burst out laughing.

"You're a brave girl!" he said. "But no, I'm not that pig. I am the Marquis, the rebel leader those of your race are afraid of."

"Well, would you look at that? And what are you rebelling against, the price of nappies?" Attica was so irritated she didn't weigh up the consequences of her words.

"You're starting to annoy me!"

"Me annoy you? I've been kidnapped with a knife in my back and then brought to this hovel with a sack on my head. I'm the one who should be annoyed!"

The Marquis stood up and left the corner. One of the candles illuminated one side of his body. He was very thin and not too tall. He was wearing tight trousers tucked into leather boots, a light smock and a black scarf tied around his neck.

"What were you doing in the cemetery?" he asked, pausing emphatically after each word.

"I went there with a friend."

"So that street urchin is a friend of yours..." he smiled. "And what's a Chiona doing with a pickpocket in Bragunde Cemetery?"

"He kidnapped me," retorted Attica. "Oh no, what's that I'm saying? You're the one who kidnapped me."

The Marquis advanced slowly until he was in front of her. It was at this point that the girl could finally see his face clearly. He can't have been more than eighteen. He had thin lips, which were still greasy from his food, and a long, slightly hooked nose. Curly hair, which he wore longer than most Malluma boys, fell to his shoulders.

I've seen that face before, thought Attica, unable to pinpoint it exactly.

The boy smiled ironically.

"Do you have her wallet?" he asked the henchman who had

79

brought her to the tavern. The man threw a brown, leather wallet to the Marquis.

"Hey, when did you take that?" asked Attica with a mixture of anger and astonishment. "So I'm the one who hangs out with pickpockets, you say..."

The Marquis opened the wallet and rummaged about inside.

"Well, look'ee who we have here!" he shouted, pulling out Attica's identity card. "Well, well, well!"

He started hopping about the girl on one foot.

"See where she lives, in the very heart of Plugufan. Looks like we've got ourselves a big one!"

He moved away from the girl and glanced at the others.

"I'm sure they'll be willing to free several of our comrades on Vendaval Island in exchange for little Miss..." he turned over the card to find out her name, "Attica..."

The surname got caught in his throat. He stared into her eyes. The girl realized he'd recognized her. The Marquis frowned in concern and, behind the mist that swirled about her memory, Attica glimpsed the face of a young child. Years back, one summer, this child had frequently come to her house in the company of his uncle, her family's Malluma gardener. The boy's name was Lopo, and he must have been a couple of years older than she was. While his uncle worked, they would play games in the back garden. In fact, despite the fact she was younger, it was she who taught him how to ride a bike.

One day, Attica heard a conversation between her mother and the gardener. The Malluma explained his sister's son hadn't had an easy life in the nabrallo. Lopo was a migas, somebody with a Malluma mother and a Gwende father. Of course, the boy had never met his father, a rich man from

Plugufan who'd taken a liking to his maid and then fired her after making her pregnant. This shame was a heavy burden for the family and for Lopo himself, who Attica remembered as a shy, withdrawn little boy, nothing like the proud, arrogant man standing in front of her.

"Hello, Lopo," she whispered in his ear, confirming the Marquis's suspicions.

The boy turned to the others in the tavern.

"Please go out for a while," he asked them.

The hinges of the door groaned once more, and they all went out, except for the woman with the ponytail, who disappeared through a door behind the bar. Despite their astonished looks, nobody dared to question the boss's orders.

"You've changed," said Lopo when they were left alone. "Last time I saw you, you were a cricket about this high."

"And you were a frightened little boy. Look at you now, a rebel leader!"

"Adapt or die, isn't that what they say?" reflected the boy absent-mindedly. "Would you like a drink?"

"Some water, please."

Lopo went through a gap under the bar, grabbed a glass from one of the shelves and filled it with tap water.

"We don't have bottled water," he said, placing a glass of murky water on top of the counter. "Such luxuries don't make it to the nabrallos."

Attica downed the whole glass without breathing. She was dying of thirst.

"Some more?"

"Yes, please."

As he served her another glass of water, Lopo brought up the subject that was bothering him.

"Listen, Attica, everybody here respects me, despite..."

"Despite the fact you're a migas," the girl interrupted him.

"That's right. Nobody here knows my father was a Chiona, and I'd like it to stay that way. There's a lot at stake, really. What we're preparing... well, it's bigger than anything done before, bigger than anything ever imagined. There are people who risk their lives on a daily basis for this, while others are rotting away in prison cells on Vendaval. It wouldn't be good if someone had the slightest doubt," Lopo's eyes were lost in the past. "Your mother was a strange woman, that's true, but she wasn't a reactionary."

"She most certainly wasn't," replied Attica sadly, remembering how long it had been since she'd heard from her.

The door behind the bar suddenly opened, and the curvy woman with the ponytail came back into the tavern. She looked worried.

"Marquis, something's wrong," she blurted out.

"Tell me," ordered Lopo.

"In front of the Chiona?"

"You can forget about her."

The woman took a few seconds to speak, still unused to the girl's awkward presence.

"Anaisusa Campia, the tanner's wife, is here. Her son's not well, he has a very high temperature."

"What can I do?" asked Lopo, visibly annoyed. "I'm not a doctor."

"The woman doesn't have the money to pay for a doctor. She went looking for Cecilio, the blind healer from Morvane Tower, but couldn't find him. It seems that old mole has been swallowed by the earth."

The woman's words reminded Attica of a sentence she'd

heard that very night: "Find a mole to follow," Onga had said. Had the witch been referring to this blind healer? Attica suddenly felt a strong desire to talk it over with Fuco, to reveal this little clue to him. She gazed at the scorpion on the ground, which the old man had crushed with the broom. "They're just a silly joke compared with the evil lurking beneath us." All this was madness! Her good sense told her to get the hell out of there, to leg it to the station and to wait for the first train leaving in the morning. "The evil lurking beneath us..."

"Is the child in a really bad way?" Lopo's question interrupted her thoughts.

"It seems so," replied the waitress.

"Then give her some money from the emergency box so he can see a doctor."

The woman with the ponytail nodded and disappeared back through the door behind the bar. The Marquis stared at Attica.

"Too much responsibility sometimes. You see what I mean?"

"Yes."

The boy headed for the door to the street and banged on it three times with his fist. A few seconds later, the door opened, and one of his henchmen poked his head in through the opening.

"We're going to let the Chiona go," announced the boss. "Take her wherever she wants to go."

The man looked as if he hadn't understood the order, or didn't agree with it, but he didn't answer back. He gestured to Attica to follow him. Lopo, the Marquis from the nabrallo of Bragunde, said goodbye to her from the doorstep. He gave her his hand, which she accepted.

"I haven't seen my uncle for quite some time. Does he still work for your mother?"

The girl nodded.

"If you see him, send him my regards."

The henchman covered Attica's head with the sack, which still reeked of petrol.

"Where do you want to go?"

"You wouldn't know how to find Fuco, the boy who was with me, would you?"

"I think I may be able to find him," replied the man before grabbing Attica's arm and guiding her through the maze of Bragunde■

A desperate miaowing from the street interrupted Mastrina's story. Night had fallen, and the light had acquired the reddish tone of caramel. I'd been shivering from the cold for quite some time, but had been too absorbed in Attica's adventures to want to go for a blanket. Now seemed a good time.

"Could you open the door to those layabouts?" asked Mastrina.

The rest had done her good, she'd even got some colour back in her cheeks.

I ran downstairs and opened the door. The cats bundled into the hallway. The last one in was the cat with the spot on its nose, which stopped to rub against my leg, purring. Its companions, meanwhile, raced silently upstairs.

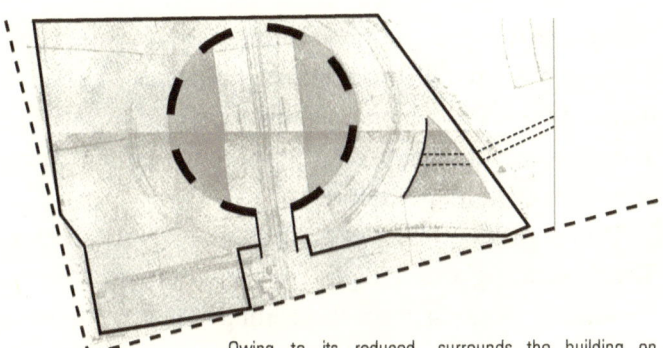

Owing to its reduced dimensions, Morvane Tower hardly ever fulfilled its original purpose as a residence. The walled enclosure is irregular in shape. There is only one entrance to the tower, which is double-locked. A ditch surrounds the building on two sides.

A popular Malluma legend tells of the existence of a passage that links the tower with the underground land of Nigrofe.

Mastrino Duardos Edrise, *Architecture, Town Planning and Figurative Art in the Nabrallo of Bragunde*

"I'm cold," I said to Mastrina when I returned upstairs.

"Me too. Do me another favour. My room is downstairs, next to the bathroom. Open the left door of the wardrobe and take two blankets from the upper shelf."

I ran back downstairs, feeling my way until I was in front of the door to her bedroom. I filled my lungs with air. I don't know why I did this. The truth is entering Mastrina's bedroom commanded my respect. It was like going up a notch in the scale of intimacy. It sounds dumb, I know, but I recall the sense of privilege I experienced that evening. Perhaps it was just a feeling of satisfaction at managing things properly for once in the intricate labyrinth of human relations.

The room was almost as small as the adjoining bathroom. The first thing that caught my attention was the metal chandelier hanging from the ceiling. There was only one bulb in its socket, the other seven arms were all empty. Austere, sober, modest… any of these adjectives would do to describe the bedroom, especially if one compared the absence of ornaments to the anarchic exuberance upstairs. Its role as a bedroom was confirmed by the presence of a tall bed flanked by two antiquated bedside tables; on the wall, a painting with the typical scene of a harvest in some isolated town of the north; and hiding the little garden that grew behind the house, two white curtains in front of a square window; the wardrobe, my objective, was a dark, wooden cupboard with no more embellishments than the golden keys in its doors.

Following Mastrina's instructions, I opened the left door and took out two blankets, one red and smooth, not very thick, the other formed by the union of dozens of little triangles of dyed worsted.

Back upstairs, I gave my teacher the red blanket and kept the multi-coloured one for myself. I sat back down on the carpet and used this opportunity to go over with the narrator some aspects of the story that were buzzing about inside my head. We talked for the sake of talking, with no desire for controversy. It was new and comforting to talk like this. It was like sweeping away all the cobwebs that teenage angst had spun inside my patience. Like being admitted to some exclusive club, far away from school and all its banalities. Nivardo? As far as I was concerned, he could carry on hanging out with his strawberry princess, I was on another level.

"I like the story, you know I do," I began, "and not just as a way of getting away from the klavia! And yet there are times when it leaves me feeling confused. What I mean is I don't know whether it forms part of your memories or you're just making it up as we go along, to keep me entertained."

"Reality or fiction?"

"That's right! For example, one of my teachers, Mr Kongare, is a fan of modern history. He's always taking us to the audiovisual room and subjecting us to these tedious documentaries about the Malluma struggle for civil rights. Well, not once have I heard mention of the Marquis of Bragunde, who you define in your story as a rebel leader."

"And you doubt his existence?"

"Not at all, that's not what I mean! I'm not exactly an expert in such matters. I spend half the class chatting with Muriel."

Mastrina spread the blanket so that it covered her feet. She looked like a gigantic caterpillar.

"Perhaps there wasn't only one Marquis, perhaps there were many," she said. "It's not the name that matters."

"I see, a different kind of pedagogy, of learning, that doesn't involve memorizing names, and all that," I scoffed good-naturedly. "Kongare's into all that nonsense as well."

"And why shouldn't he be? We can learn from

everything, but don't think my purpose is to guide you in life or anything like that."

"So why are you doing it? Why waste your time telling me this story?'

"I'm not wasting my time, I enjoy the story and your company," she confided. "Stop wondering whether it really happened or not, whether I heard the story or am making it up, because I can't tell you and I don't want to. Besides, this may sound a little manic, but that would break the magic spell that enables the story to function."

"The magic you promised me on the first day..." I laughed.

Mastrina also let out a laugh, which descended into a bout of coughing that convulsed her body.

"There's something else that worries me," I said once the coughing had died down, "and that's whether we're heading anywhere or we're just jumping about from one place to another without any real..."

"Direction?"

"That's right."

The old woman got up from her rocking chair and walked to the little table.

"Would you like another piece of cisté?" she asked.

"Are you going to have one?"

"No, I'm not. I have the impression I ate too much today."

She silently cut another piece of the cake and offered it to me. I started eating it slowly, savouring each mouthful. It really was very succulent.

"You're a clever girl, Guiomar," she declared, having retaken her seat.

"What makes you say that?"

"You've just posed the forbidden question, but using other words."

"It makes you think," I said, my mouth full of tasty cisté. I swallowed and continued, "To what extent is it credible? I don't mean what happens, rather… let me explain. Have you ever seen the adventures of Inspector Lepakke?" Mastrina shook her head. She seemed intrigued by this new topic. "Well, it's this crazy TV series which has been running longer than man has been upright. The main character, this hard-boiled detective, finds himself at the end of each episode being captured or in a situation where his life is in danger. 'Will Lepakke be able to repel the attack of the giant spider?' 'Will Lepakke survive the onslaught of poisoned darts?' Of course he will!" I swallowed another mouthful. "And yet you're always left with the desire to see how the good old inspector will escape the mortal danger, it's what makes the story work. That is what I mean."

"Perhaps we older people are simply more used to this kind of structure," reasoned the old woman. "I don't wish to sound pessimistic or overly transcendental, but I think life is defined by the way we overcome a succession of fears."

I finished the sweet and put my plate on the table.

"Is there something that causes you real fear, great terror?" I asked out of curiosity.

"Of course there is!' replied the old lady, her eyes open wide. "I can't bear dark, enclosed spaces."

First light, which had already delineated the gentle hills in the east, had also emptied the railway tunnel and silenced its uproar. The metal drums that had warmed the party now emitted nothing more than smoke inside the enormous stone hole.

The Marquis's henchman pulled off the sack and pointed to an old car in the distance that had been propped up on some planks. As he spoke, the first train on the circular line went creaking over the rails, drowning out his words.

"What did you say?" asked the girl.

"The boy's inside the boot."

The man turned and walked away, whistling the tune of some melancholy hicupé.

Attica approached the car and pressed her ear against the boot. She could hear this dull, regular sound coming from under the lid. Fuco was snoring away peacefully. She had to put up a fight with the rusty lock before it released its contents. The light and noise woke up the boy, who stretched his swollen limbs outside his cell.

"I've slept in worse places," he joked. "At least there was no way for those ugly bugs to get in here."

Attica couldn't help smiling when she saw the street urchin yawn and scratch his head, just like any other boy preparing to have breakfast after getting out of bed. The thought of breakfast sent her stomach into a frenzy. How long had it been since she'd eaten? She hadn't ingested anything since lunch the previous day and, what with the nervous state she'd been in about the journey and the concert, that hadn't been a large amount.

"Are you feeling hungry?" she asked Fuco.

"I'm famished," replied the boy.

"Do you know somewhere where we could have some breakfast?"

"That depends on whether you have some ready cash."

"I have a little."

Along the way, Attica told him all about her short-lived captivity.

"You were lucky," intoned Fuco seriously, "the Marquis's lot are pretty heavy-handed. That wouldn't be the first time I've had a beating for sticking my nose into their business."

They had breakfast in the kitchen of a private house. An old woman charged them an entrance fee and told them to wait their turn in the corridor, in a queue with some other people. Breakfast consisted of a concoction of cornmeal and sour milk, which Attica found revolting, but seeing the anxiety with which the other diners wolfed it down, she didn't dare protest. Nobody let up for a moment. Fuco practically had his nose inside the bowl. That bit about being famished wasn't a joke, thought the girl.

When they'd finished, a new group entered the kitchen. Out in the street, Fuco pulled up his jersey to reveal a round, distended stomach beneath prominent ribs. He patted his belly button and smiled in satisfaction.

"Life always looks better with a full belly," he declared. "Now, what dragons did you say we had to slay?"

Attica covered her head with the hood of her coat and stopped in front of the boy.

"Listen, have you ever heard of a healer called Cecilio?" she asked him.

"Of course I have! Everybody in Bragunde knows Cecilio. Who told you about him? I warn you he's a bit loopy."

"In the bar where I was taken, a woman referred to him as 'that old mole.' And what did Onga tell us? To follow the mole that knows the way."

"It's a coincidence," said Fuco, lighting a cigarette. "Old mole, blind man, squinty... they're just figures of speech."

Attica kicked an enormous white scorpion with the toe of her boot.

"I don't think it's just a coincidence," she reflected with her hands in her pockets. "Onga didn't look to me as if she was just talking for the sake of talking."

"Perhaps not," replied Fuco. "All the same, I wouldn't give it too much importance. 'The evil lurking beneath us,' remember that? It's just an old wives' tale. My grandma used to spend the whole day wittering on about Nigrofe, the lost city, the great hope... All drivel."

Attica took the cigarette out of his mouth and threw it to the ground. Before Fuco could protest, she said:

"Let's go."

"Where to?"

"To that tower place."

"Morvane Tower? What about your train?"

"Trains run every day."

They headed east along the main avenue. The nabrallo was a hive of activity again, having woken up from the previous night. The stalls of fruit, vegetables and other foodstuffs filled the pavements, and white sheets shone in the warm rays of the sun, hanging from the balconies of little houses. The horns and engines of vehicles advancing chaotically over the potholed surface drowned out any other noise that morning. From time to time, they would glimpse a SAN patrol, which they would avoid by hiding behind a stall until the danger had passed.

"Tell me about this tower," Attica asked Fuco.

"There's not much I can say, only what I heard about it as a child."

"As a child? Crikey, that must have been ages ago..." mocked Attica.

"You know what I mean! Morvane was a wealthy Chiona businessman. He was married to an aristocrat from Plugufan, who was richer than he was. Everything perfect, you might have thought. Not at all. The couple couldn't have any children, and Morvane started hanging out with this beautiful Malluma by the name of Arcadia-Lupa. So the legend goes, it was this lover of Morvane's who put a spell on his wife and made her sterile. Arcadia-Lupa was deeply into the Subteran cult – you know, that business about the monastery and the tree..."

Attica had failed to understand this last bit, as was clear from the expression on her face.

"You don't have any idea what I'm talking about, do you?" said Fuco. The girl shook her head. "Ah well, it doesn't matter. It's just an old wives' tale. The fact is this pretty witch was obsessed with the idea of reaching Nigrofe, so she got Morvane to build her a tower where her studies told her the entrance to the lost world was situated. That's about all I can tell you."

Fuco had been entertaining himself by throwing pebbles at half a dozen noisy felines on heat, which earned him a severe reprimand from an old woman in a floral headscarf. Attica, meanwhile, endeavoured to process this torrent of information, oblivious to the scandal between the old woman and the boy.

The eastern side of the nabrallo of Bragunde gave way to a landscape crowned by rocky hills. Perched on one of the highest was Morvane Tower, constructed out of large blocks of dull stone, on one of which there was a lightning conductor. An unassailable wall stretched from the sides of the tower, two arms enveloping an inner courtyard. What was noticeable about the building was the absence of windows, the impression of its being a solid prism of stone broken only by vertical slits in the walls. The courtyard was linked to the outside world by an arch with an iron gate.

"It's open, how strange," said Fuco in surprise.

Attica, exhausted from the climb up the hill, was barely able to string two words together. From the summit, the nabrallo was an unending sea of withered rooftops.

They entered the courtyard, which was round and dark. In the centre was a well with a little red roof and a rope attached to a pulley wheel. The ground was formed by the rocky summit on which the tower stood. In a corner was a wooden hut, little more than a shed thatched with palm leaves.

A white, filthy, matted dog suddenly emerged from the hut and ran towards them. The children scrambled up the iron gate to be out of its reach, but the dog's intentions were not violent. It lay on the ground, beneath their feet, and started whining mournfully.

"It doesn't look so dangerous," whispered Attica.

"No, it doesn't," agreed Fuco. "You go down first."

"Coward!"

The girl came down from her refuge and bent to stroke the dog's back, which it appreciated by licking her hand.

"It's Cecilio's dog," said the boy, on the ground by now, "so the old fellow can't be too far away."

And yet, however carefully they checked Morvane Tower, they couldn't find any trace of the canine's owner.

"Well, that's a mystery!" exclaimed Fuco in the courtyard, as he tried unsuccessfully to get the dog to fetch a stick he was throwing.

"Let's look for a way down," suggested Attica.

"A way down where?"

The girl didn't reply. She climbed some iron bars stuck in the rock to the tower's entrance, which was on a level with the top of the wall, and entered the enormous stone enclosure. She went down a ramp to the lower floor, which was shrouded in complete darkness. Her heart was beating furiously. It didn't take Fuco long to arrive.

"You can't see a thing down here," he murmured as soon as he set foot on the rocky surface. The blue of the sky could be glimpsed through a crack in the wall, which was barely enough to let a ray through or illuminate even the tiniest chip of stone.

"Use your lighter," said Attica.

The flickering flame lit up the children's faces. They scanned the ground and all four corners of the room, but couldn't find any sign of a trapdoor, tunnel or staircase that might take them downwards.

"Let's go and have another look in the courtyard," suggested the girl. But they didn't have much luck there, either.

Suddenly Cecilio's white dog stopped following them meekly around and, vigorously wagging its tail, positioned itself in front of the well. It placed its front paws on the circular wall and started barking. The well acted as a resonance tube, and the dog's barks echoed wildly around the courtyard. Attica and Fuco approached the edge of the hole. The boy grabbed the pulley rope.

"It won't turn, it's stuck, as if someone had manipulated it in order to go down," he said.

He climbed on to the wall and, grabbing hold of the rope with his hands and legs, started descending. When he reached the bottom, he set foot on dry ground and was surprised at the absence of water. He felt the ground, which was made up of smooth, hexagonal stones. He took out his lighter and turned it on. One of the stones wasn't properly sealed. He calculated that someone who wasn't too fat could fit through the opening.

"How's it going down there?" cried Attica from the mouth of the tube.

"Well, it's an odd sort of well," replied Fuco. "Send down the sturdiest stick you can find."

The girl dropped down a long, pointed stick she located in the pile of firewood by the shed. The boy sharpened the point a little more with his knife and stuck it in the gap next to the stone to act as a lever. He pushed with all his might, but the stick only ended up breaking, without the stone having moved an inch.

Fuco gave up and sat on the ground. He took advantage of Attica's absence to have a quiet smoke. On lighting his cigarette, something caught his attention: in the stones that enclosed the cavity, he came across an opening in the form of a scorpion. It must have been about the length of his little finger – he hadn't noticed it first time round because of its small size. He brought the flame and his eye close to the hole, but could only make out more darkness.

Then, suddenly, the ground started shaking under his feet. Fuco leaped up and pressed himself as hard as he could against the stone wall. The hexagonal stone he'd tried unsuccessfully to move was now sinking. It then shifted slowly to one side, revealing a large, black hole. Out of the darkness came a cry, and then a pair of hands grabbed hold of the edge.

Fuco helped the man to climb into the well and sat him on the ground, resting his back against the wall. It was Cecilio. His bald pate was sprinkled with beads of sweat that ran down his forehead and into his eyes. He moaned softly, a lament Fuco was unable to comprehend. He lit his lighter again and observed the blind man's body.

"What's going on?" inquired Attica from the top of the well.

"Cecilio's turned up!" replied the urchin. "He's badly wounded■"

The sound of silence took the place of Mastrina's voice. We were sheltering in the placid shadows of the klavia room, which glistened in the light of the harvest moon like a white, motionless ghost. In one corner of the balcony, the cats were nothing more than a bleary, inert shadow.

"It's night already," remarked Mastrina.

"Is it time to go?" I asked, hiding my displeasure at the passage of time.

"It's time to rest, little girl. This old body is crying out for bed."

I said goodbye to the old lady and emerged on to Bagare Street, which was deserted and serenely lit. In the windows of the wooden houses, very few lights were still working. A shiver of cold penetrated my body and forced me to run. I had arranged to speak to Muriel on the phone, but preferred not to. I didn't feel like talking to anybody that night.

Xenevra Ianique:

THE STORY OF A MYTH

Other sports enable female players from humble districts to live with all the finesse of a privileged area. With maila, it's the exact opposite: this sport permits the heiresses of the finest families in Audierna to behave for an hour and a half like veritable beasts.

There is just one way to fight the cold when it penetrates your body so much you can feel it in the marrow of your bones, and that is to get under a shower that is as hot as you can bear and then wait patiently until three spasms indicate the inveterate cold has been banished from your flesh. This was the advice of a maternal great-uncle, a sluggish, overweight man who had apparently been a famous hero in the wars of the north. I hardly knew him, to tell the truth, and so I always pictured him posing imperishably and smiling stupidly in a military uniform covered in medals on the wall of our family's living room.

That Monday, having sloshed around a muddy maila pitch for more than an hour, I followed my great-uncle's instructions to the letter. With my body now warm, I got dressed, said goodbye to my teammates and boarded an empty bus that left me in front of our house. I would normally have walked back from training, but that afternoon I was aching all over. It had been a good session.

As I was putting on my pyjamas in my room, somebody knocked at the door. It was my brother, who waited patiently on the landing for me to open.

"What do you want?" I said a little harshly.

"How was training?" In between sentences, he blew bubbles with his chewing gum, which made me really nervous.

"OK."

"Are you going to play on Sunday?"

Ignoring this last question, I pricked his bubble with my finger and closed the door, returning to the intimacy of my bedroom.

I adore my brother and today we're very close, but things were different back then. He may just have been a repugnant, know-it-all child, which was how I saw him. Or else the problem resided with my own unsociable character. Perhaps it was a combination of both those circumstances, at least that's what the distance tells me after all these years.

The fact is he knocked on the door again and I opened like a whirlwind.

"May I know what the hell it is you want?" I roared angrily.

My brother blew another bubble and then burst it, covering his face with a mint-green film.

"Your klavia teacher called," he said, enjoying being in possession of privileged information.

"And…"

"She's sick, so you won't have a lesson tomorrow. That's a stroke of luck, isn't it?" he remarked, but this last attempt at complicity ended up with the door slamming in his face as well.

The following day, I ignored his warning and, coming out of school, headed back down 15 August Avenue, a long arrow that passes right through my quarter before sticking in the skin of old Plugufan.

When I reached the little, white house, I instinctively brought my forefinger up to the bell, but fortunately restrained the impulse before making it ring. If Mastrina was sick, she'd probably be in bed. It seemed somehow cruel to make her get up and open the door.

I walked around the house to the back. There, enclosed by a hedge, lay a small, square garden brimming with flowers and fruit bushes.

The curtain in Mastrina's room was drawn and, however hard I strained my eyes, trying to focus my vision, I couldn't make out more than a collection of immobile shadows inside. In my confusion, I decided to try the back door, and surprisingly it opened. In the silent corridor, I felt like an intruder and advanced on tiptoe, which was a little absurd. At some point, in some way, I would have to make my presence known. After hesitating for a while, I decided to do this in the simplest way possible: by knocking at the door of her room. First softly, almost in a panic. Then, having got silence as the only response, a little more vigorously.

"Who is it?" I heard Mastrina ask on the other side of the door. She spoke in a tiny voice, though she didn't sound afraid.

"Guiomar."

"Come in."

She invited me to sit at the foot of the bed. Her hair was down, spread over the pillow like a white flame, and her shoulders were covered by a thick, woollen shawl.

"You look startled," she smiled at me. "Is my appearance so awful?"

On the bedside table, I could see a tray with the remains of a meal. She appeared to read my mind.

"Old Mastrina isn't as alone as you thought."

"I never thought anything," I replied a little shamefacedly.

The rest had done her good, she said, and, despite her

fragile appearance, she was in a happy mood. She asked me to go upstairs and switch on the record player. I climbed the stairs and bumped into the cats. They viewed me with contempt for a moment, but then immediately closed their eyes and went on with their siesta.

I took a record off the shelf at random. It turned out to be *Trace of Giants* by Messengers of Hicupé. Mastrina congratulated me on my selection. I was tempted to hide the random nature of my choice in order to claim a musical knowledge I was now desperately keen to acquire.

I sat again at the foot of her bed, and we listened to the music. The mattress was as hard as a rock. Mastrina enjoyed the quick music, her glassy eyes hidden behind her eyelids. For a moment, I thought she was asleep, but then, without prior warning, she decided to resume our story.

"How are we going to get him out of there?" shouted Attica. It was obvious she was nervous, and Fuco couldn't find a suitable answer to calm her down.

"How should I know?" he retorted. "I thought you were the brains and I was the brawn."

"What's that you're muttering?"

"Oh nothing, forget it."

The boy weighed up the few possibilities offered by the narrow well. Cecilio had stopped moaning and was now lying with his head resting on his shoulder. Blood poured from his right thigh. From the edge of the well, the dog could be heard whining away in concern at its owner's condition.

Fuco came up with an idea. He wasn't overly hopeful it would work, but he had to think of something. He grabbed the rope and put it around the chest of the wounded man, tying it under his arms.

"Try and unblock the pulley!" he cried to Attica.

The girl struggled with the mechanism for a couple of minutes and finally managed to extract the iron bolt that had stopped it working.

"It's OK now!" she told the boy.

"Good. OK. When I tell you, pull on the rope. Try and do so strongly, but without jerking. You can start now."

The girl grabbed the rope and started pulling, leaning backwards to enlist her own body weight. From below, Fuco helped by pushing Cecilio's body as far as his arms could reach. When this help finished, however, Attica was unable to carry on lifting the dead weight. She gave up, and the old man's body sank slowly back to the bottom of the well. Fuco scratched his head in frustration.

"Block the pulley again!"

He climbed the rope until he was outside. He then released the mechanism again.

"How do you think he managed to climb down the rope?" wondered Attica.

"What I'd like to know is how he was planning to come back up again..." remarked the boy. "Let's try between the two of us. We'll do it slowly so he doesn't bang into the walls."

They grabbed the rope and started lifting the body with short, synchronized pulls that prevented the blind man being harmed during the ascent. There was a moment of concern, but in the end they managed to rescue him from the hole. They carried him to the hut in the corner of the courtyard and laid him down on a straw mattress. Attica gazed at him in silence. He was a tall man with a broad forehead and a line of curly, grey hair that connected his temples behind his head. He had a bulbous nose and fat lips surrounded by stubble. He was wearing some thick, blue dungarees and a white smock that was drenched in sweat.

The dog affectionately licked its master's hands. When it sensed the gravity of the situation, it collapsed at the foot of the bed and lay there, motionless.

"Now what?" asked Fuco.

"We have to bind that wound," said Attica, rummaging through the stuff in the shed until she found a pile of crumpled clothes in a box. She pulled out a white shirt, which she proceeded to tear into strips. She then lifted up Cecilio's trouser leg. The wound didn't look good, the red of the blood mixed with the black of the clots.

"Damn, it's infected," said the girl.

"How on earth did he do that?" asked Fuco in fear. "They look like the marks of some enormous teeth."

Attica went back to the pile of stuff beneath the palm roof.

"We need antibiotics," she moaned uneasily.

"I don't know what that is," replied Fuco, "but I'm quite sure you're not going to find it here■"

"Why don't they take him to the doctor?"

My sudden question took Mastrina by surprise. She used this short pause to drink a sip of water.

"Let us continue," she said, placing the glass back on the bedside table.

"**W**hy don't we take him to the doctor?" suggested Attica. "This is a nabrallo, remember? Even breathing here costs money."

"I have money," said the girl, pulling a couple of notes and some coins out of the inner pocket of her coat.

"Real money," declared Fuco with an embittered gesture.

Feeling powerless, the girl leaned against the plank wall and gazed at the blind man's contorted face.

"He has a fever."

Cecilio writhed on the mattress. First, he rubbed his chest with his arms, as if trying to repel the attack of an army of imaginary insects. He then started emitting a series of incomprehensible sounds. The two children went over and strained their ears, trying to decipher some of the words.

"...treasure...treasure...stolen...the brothers...disappeared... treasure... pay..."

Fuco and Attica glanced at each other, hoping the other would understand.

"What's he talking about?" asked the girl.

"A treasure stolen by some brothers?" ventured the boy.

In a corner of the hut, there was a bucket full of water. Attica grabbed one of the strips left over from the bandage, dipped it in the bucket and placed it on Cecilio's forehead. Every now and then, whenever the cloth got too hot, she would dip it in the water again to keep it fresh.

The old man finally stopped being delirious and fell into a deep sleep. When he woke up, night had fallen over the nabrallo. Fuco had lit an oil lamp, which filled the inside of the hut with a yellow glow. Attica was sitting on the floor, nodding off from time to time, exhausted by the series of adventures she had experienced since setting foot in Bragunde.

"Who are you?" asked Cecilio in a broken voice when he came to.

"My name is Barucus Fuco, and I'm the son of Dantus Baruc the Firewalker."

"And the Chiona?"

Attica leaped up, surprised by the blind man's question.

"How did you know she's a Chiona?" inquired Fuco.

Cecilio endeavoured to laugh, but his guffaw turned into a low lament.

"How else?" he said finally. "By the smell."

The girl came over to the bed and placed her hand on his forehead. His temperature had gone down considerably, but he still had a fever.

"My name is Attica," she introduced herself. "You have a serious wound on your leg."

"That would explain this terrible pain..." groaned the man.

"How did you get it?" asked Fuco.

Cecilio fell silent. His white, distracted eyes shone under a thin film of tears. Attica insisted.

"We took you out of the well. Where had you been?"

"I can't remember."

"When you were delirious, you talked about a treasure and some brothers," intervened Fuco.

"I don't know what you mean," replied the old man, looking very uncomfortable. "It must have been a bad dream."

A sack hanging from a nail contained a few crusts of stale bread, which they shared out between them. Cecilio barely ate two mouthfuls before falling asleep again because of the fever, which had gone back up to a dangerous level.

"We have to do something," whispered Attica in concern.

"Yes, but what?" replied a confused Fuco.

"Let's ask Onga for help."

The boy opened his eyes wide at this proposal.

"You want us to go back to that sinister cemetery in search of that witch? You must be out of your mind..."

"No!!" replied Attica, speaking all the time in a low voice. "That's not what I mean. We can't leave Cecilio on his own. I meant for me to stay here while *you* go back to the cemetery."

"Why me?"

"Are you serious? Because I don't know the nabrallo."

The ragamuffin finally accepted his mission. Muttering under his breath, he stowed away his fear and left Morvane Tower, going south all the while, in the direction of the stony fields on the outskirts of the nabrallo.

After two hours of sitting at the foot of Cecilio's bed, silence had pushed Attica to the brink of desperation. She finally heard some footsteps on the rocky ground of the courtyard. In came Fuco first, leading the way, and then Onga, and the bald giant who seemed to accompany her everywhere. The Queen of the Cemetery had an enormous leather bag hanging from her shoulder. With every step she took, the beads around her neck jangled. Without even saying hello, she walked to the bed and stared at Cecilio. For a few moments, perhaps on account of the oil lamp's mellifluous light, Onga's eyes seemed to acquire the texture of igneous rock.

"Wait outside, wait," she ordered the children.

Fuco and Attica whiled away the time, sitting silently on the rocky summit, which acted as an impassive guard to the tower's entrance. Bragunde was an ocean of darkness, which continued monotonously as far as the next nabrallo, Zambela. Only on the right, northwards, did the distant gleam of the Gwende districts on the other side of the River Ioke illuminate the horizon.

Their hearts leaped when they realized someone had sat down next to them. Onga had crept up silently, accompanied by a light breeze that caressed their skin.

"He won't die from this, he won't," she declared solemnly. The children smiled with satisfaction in the shadows.

"Is he awake?" asked Attica.

Onga fixed her with her beady eyes.

"Your presence disturbs me, Chiona," the witch suddenly spat, although the harshness of her words conveyed not reproach, but astonishment. "Yes, he's awake, and I've just spoken to him about you two. I would like to know what arcane entity fixed its choice on you two, I would."

Onga grabbed them by the arm, sticking her blackened nails into their skin. She rolled her eyes until they became white.

"I had a revelation, I had. The tree, its heart rotten, wept tears of fire on my naked skin. Despite the pain, I could hear its lament, I could. Every tear it exuded drew your faces in the warm air. I didn't want to believe it, but its words were clear.

Of pale face
and fearful race
they came from the north
with bloody hunger,

with spears,
swords,
knives
and daggers.

Branch of this tree,
renewed seed,

iron in the face,
disdainful gaze.

Yellow,
courageous,
rational
and senseless.

Clever boy,
son of good stock,
fights at her side
in the gaping hole.

They're the ones,
they're the ones,
they're the ones,
they're the ones.

The two children gazed at Onga's ecstasy as if at an exotic spectacle, frightened and amazed at the same time. They didn't understand anything and yet couldn't bring themselves to formulate any questions in a natural way. Fuco coughed, clearing his throat and preparing to break the old woman's trance.

"They're the ones... who are they? Who are we?"

Onga's eyes regained their normal, black colour.

"You are our saviours■"

In the beginning, the heart of the earth was only matter subsumed in silence. Later, the particles began to move apart, emitting a sound. By means of this movement, the luminous particles rose up, forming the inner sky, which is called Chiela-Ebenaxo. The other particles that didn't rise up formed the ground of an immense cavity, which is called Nigrofe.

Malnovan Logo

"This tastes awful!" protested Cecilio, sitting up in bed, when Attica, Fuco and Onga re-entered the hut. He was holding a smoking bowl with an insipid, whitish broth inside. Onga ignored his complaints and, leaning on her stick, went over to the bald giant. The man, as he'd done the previous night, was nodding off, sitting in a corner of the shed. The old woman took his hand and traced a few signs on the palm with the nail of her little finger. This must have been the way they communicated because, without needing any further explanations, the man left the hut, walked across the courtyard to the entrance arch and disappeared into the nabrallo's metallic moonlight.

Onga came over to Cecilio's bed and had a look at his leg. There was a large, black scar on his thigh, which had been smothered with a poultice of earth and herbs. Despite the horror it caused the children, the fact is the wound looked much better and the swelling in the leg had gone down considerably.

"Drink it down to the last drop, drink," commanded the old witch. "If I give it to you, it's because it's good."

Cecilio lifted the bowl to his lips, without hiding his distaste for the murky beverage.

"I suppose I should thank you," he said to the void. Attica and Fuco remained silent, not knowing what to say. They were still overwhelmed by Onga's recent trance, endeavouring to assume the new and disconcerting role of "saviours" that some mystical providence wished to give them. Cecilio interpreted their silence.

"Have you spoken to them already?" he asked the old woman.

"A little," she replied laconically.

The blind man continued struggling with the wonder-working poison for a while longer. Onga waited at the end of the bed, sitting there stiffly, not even blinking.

"Tell them," insisted Cecilio.

"There isn't much time for talking, there isn't."

"Well, they should know. We can't send them down there blind. Not even I, with all my knowledge, was able to prevent this misfortune," he signalled his leg. "Imagine what will happen to those two children without help."

Onga listened warily, not moving a single muscle on her face. She looked like a statue sculpted out of dark wood. She was silent for a minute before speaking.

"The universe is a succession of delicate balances: day and night, earth and sky, fire and water... Everything has its opposite, its natural reverse, that helps to define all the things we know. What we cannot perceive naturally functions in the same way, what we cannot perceive. These two worlds, the earthly and the immaterial, coexist in a kind of harmony. They are, if you wish, the two sides of a single coin, the two sides."

Fuco nudged Attica in the ribs to elicit her sympathy at the torrent of strange words he was finding it difficult to process. But Attica was entranced by the old woman, in search of a beacon that would shed some light in all that darkness.

"The Subteran cult is based on balance," continued Onga. "The Malluma race professes the faith of its ancestors, which claims equality in the scales between good and evil. This balance is reflected in its two sacred symbols: Dendria, the peach tree, represented good, while to Tartarus fell the mission of embodying evil, death that lies in wait, conscious of its victory, death. These two symbols lived side by side in Nigrofe, their balance maintained by the priests of Venquinta Monastery."

Onga fell silent for a while, perhaps wondering how best to continue.

"Do you know the story of this tower?" she asked the children.

"More or less," replied Fuco hesitatingly.

"What kind of answer is that, you fool?" Onga grew angry.

Fuco explained what he knew about Morvane Tower, what he'd told Attica that morning.

"The word that sums up this whole story is 'obsession,' the word," reflected Onga, "an obsession that was so great it ended up turning into a disease of the soul.

"Arcadia-Lupa was, like me, a Subteran priestess. But her pride and ambition turned her into an enemy of everything our culture stands for. It was many centuries ago when Astor erected this rocky caprice for his lover, it was. He endowed it with a garrison of mercenaries for its protection, and slaves to dig a tunnel. Arcadia-Lupa's studies pointed to this place as the most suitable for reaching Nigrofe and, having dug for several years, she managed to get there, specifically to the Forest of Sanctapersico.

"In a clearing of the forest, she came across Dendria, the sacred Malluma symbol. There she prayed and fasted for more than a week, giving thanks to her ancestors for this glorious outcome to her endeavours. She lay prostrate on the ground in front of the tree, which shone majestically, its leaves reflecting the verdant glow of Nigrofe's colossal roof, the verdant glow. On the night Arcadia-Lupa returned to Audierna, she conceived a daughter by Astor. But madness had already taken hold of her brain and the poison of Dendria's beauty had completely infected her soul. The following morning, she went back down to Nigrofe with two mercenaries and stole the sacred tree, which she ordered to be transplanted to the summit of Morvane Tower. She then invited the mercenaries to drink poisoned wine, killing them so no one else would know her secret, no one else.

"Arcadia-Lupa spent the nine months of her pregnancy at the foot of the peach tree. Only Astor was permitted to visit her at the top of the tower. Every night, he would ascend for a couple of minutes to take his lover food, every night. Day after day, the Chiona tried to get her to come down, but the woman wouldn't leave Dendria's side. She gave birth there to a beautiful girl with dark hair and eyes as clear as the August sky, whom she named Aurea. Astor adored this little migas from the moment he saw her in her mother's embrace.

"Arcadia-Lupa had bewitched Astor's wife, a noble Chiona, so she wouldn't be able to have children. The wealthy businessman appointed her heiress of all his possessions, of all. This was too much for the Council of Elders that ruled Audierna at that time, on which sat Astor's father-in-law. They swore to do everything in their hands to prevent this outrage, they swore. And yet the rich businessman's power was so great the Council could hardly do anything while he was still alive.

"Then Arcadia-Lupa's madness gave rise to another misfortune. When Aurea was still a babe at the breast, a beautiful peach appeared, hanging from one of Dendria's branches. The tree produced only one fruit every three hundred and fifty-eight years, and Arcadia-Lupa understood this to be an offering from her ancestors for the birth of her daughter. It would have been better if she had studied the sacred texts with eyes of wisdom, not greed, it would. The woman took the fruit and offered it to Astor. The two lovers ate the fabulous flesh of the peach together, leaving only the stone, which was made of gold. And yet the ambitious Malluma didn't realize the pulp of Dendria's fruits contained the deadliest of poisons. The couple died that very night in each other's arms, under the sacred tree, which glowed like silver beneath the full moon of Audierna.

"Aurea was dispossessed of all her rights by the Council, and the tower was sacked by Chiona troops. But that was the least of the evils brought about by Arcadia-Lupa's decisions, the least. The theft of the tree disrupted the balance in Nigrofe, and ever since then Tartarus, the Great Evil, has been without opposition, plunging the inhabitants of the Green Country into a continuous cycle of sacrifices to satiate its greed."

When Onga had finished her explanations, she turned to stone again. It was as if she had stopped breathing.

"And the tree?" asked Attica, causing the old witch to return to the land of the living.

"Far away from Nigrofe, the tree died at the top of the tower," replied Onga. "Its remains were taken to a safe place. Last night, you were in their presence, last night. The tree now rests in the cemetery, in front of the entrance to my crypt, but its protective power has vanished■"

I turned on the light in the corridor and entered the kitchen. From the cupboard above the sink, I took out a red kettle whose paint was somewhat chipped on the spout. I filled it with water from the tap and heated it on the stove. While waiting for the water to boil, I glimpsed a shadow bustling about on the other side of the window. I crept over, a little afraid. All I could see outside was the leaves of the old oak dancing in the wind.

When the water had boiled, I dropped in two tea bags. I looked for a mug in the cupboards and found one that was white with gaudy flowers on the sides and a golden rim where the lips would go. It was ancient and fairly ugly, by the way, but for some reason its anachronism struck me as fascinating, another ticket this house in Plugufan was offering me to travel to the past. I gazed at it for a while, until again a shadow disturbed the darkness in the street. This time, I glimpsed two faces staring in through the glass. Having been discovered, they fled into the night.

I was so shocked the mug fell out of my hands and smashed on the floor, breaking into a thousand pieces.

"I broke a mug," I confessed a little later, while serving Mastrina tea in bed.

"Don't worry," she absolved me in a quiet voice.

"There were some children peeping in through the window. I got a real fright."

Mastrina laughed.

"Oh, those are my admirers! The few children left in this district are of the opinion that this house is haunted, so obviously that makes me the witch. The fact I don't go out much only adds to these rumours."

"You always have the blinds open. You should close them."

"Oh no! Leave them as they are. That would be like depriving the house of its sight."

I sat down next to her, leaning against the tall, wooden bedhead. Mastrina drank a sip of tea. She liked it to be without sugar, strong and bitter.

"Shall we go on?"

I nodded enthusiastically.

Once Onga had finished her explanation, she again mentally left the hut, sitting stiffly at the foot of the bed. It was Fuco who resolved to break the silence.

"And what is it we're supposed to do, kill that old Tartarus?"

At this point, Onga shot to her feet and whacked the boy so hard his chin collided with his chest. Fuco didn't dare complain, though he did vigorously rub the back of his neck to ease the pain. The Queen of the Cemetery sat down again and sank back into her deep lethargy.

Cecilio sat up in bed, shifting his bottom with a painful gesture so it was at the head of the bed.

"Young people, green wood..." he remarked casually. Then, in a more serious tone, he continued, "Your mission is easy to comprehend, but difficult to carry out. Listen carefully because everything you hear now may prove to be useful.

"As Onga explained, the theft of the tree upset the balance in Nigrofe. Ever since then, its people have been subjected to cruel sacrifices in order to placate Tartarus, the Great Evil. Not long ago, two brothers named Dinis and Vinicius arrived at Venquinta Monastery. They asked to see Colonel Touro, the current governor of the Green Country. Touro is not a pleasant man, nor is he overly interested in protocol, which meant the outsiders had to wait a week before he would give them an audience. These brothers claimed to have a definitive solution that would rid the land of Nigrofe of Tartarus. The Colonel, worried about the fearful creature's next visit, decided to take a risk and ordered the brothers to put their plan into action. Having received an advance for their work, Dinis and Vinicius erected a strange obelisk in the monastery courtyard, which, they said, was the balm this punished land needed.

"For many years, Touro has kept all the women of Nigrofe prisoner in the cells of Venquinta Monastery. Nobody knows the real reason. One night, while on guard, a couple of soldiers discovered Vinicius sawing away at the bars of the cell where the youngest women were held. Rumour has it he was dressed up as a woman. This sent the Colonel into a rage. He refused to pay the brothers any more money and gave them a single day to abandon those lands he rules with an iron fist.

"But Dinis and Vinicius weren't just prepared to drop the matter. They claimed to have stopped the obelisk working and so eradicated its protective power. Threatening to leave it as it is until they are paid in full, they hid themselves somewhere in Nigrofe.

"Colonel Touro is a proud man and refuses to settle the debt. The worst thing is Tartarus's moment is fast approaching. Day after day, the earth in the Green Country shakes, prophesying future ills. The abundance of scorpions heading there from all directions is just another symptom of a much more dangerous disease.

"As the only descendant of the line of Aurea and Arcadia-Lupa, I carry in my blood the blame for my ancestor's actions. Our family has kept the gold stones Dendria produced every three hundred and fifty-eight years for generations. Clinging to the hope espoused by Dinis and Vinicius, I went down to Nigrofe with this treasure, prepared to pay off two debts: the one Colonel Touro incurred with the two brothers, and the one I inherited through Arcadia-Lupa's lack of responsibility. But no sooner had I set foot in the Forest of Sanctapersico than I was savagely set upon and, worst of all, the treasure was stolen. This is where your mission begins."

The scant light thrown by the oil lamp, hanging from a hook above the bed, forced the children to strain their eyes so they could see the changing expressions on the blind man's face. Fuco rummaged in his trouser pocket and stroked the grips on his knife in an attempt to bring about a calm he didn't feel. Attica swallowed with difficulty. All this was madness, a terrible joke someone was playing on them, for which these two ragged characters – the blind man and the witch – were just some actors who'd learned their parts well.

"Are you trying to tell me the fate of Audierna rests on me and this here pickpocket?" asked Attica, pointing at Fuco. "I'm just a girl who came to Bragunde to attend a concert. I've no idea how I got mixed up in all this affair. This isn't my place, and these aren't my problems."

"I'm afraid I agree with the Chiona," remarked Fuco. "This adventure requires a different kind of hero."

Onga fixed them with the intensity of her stare.

"Then everything is lost, everything," she declared. "There are no other heroes, the mysteries were quite clear. But you are the ones who have to choose your own destiny, and not the other way round."

The white dog scratched its ear with its back paw. For a while, this was the only sound in the hut. Fuco continued stroking his knife nervously. Attica, for her part, clenched her fists, wondering which path to take.

"Tell us what we have to do," she said finally. Her determination had a positive effect on Fuco, who puffed up his chest in a willingness to accept his destiny.

Cecilio took his stick off the ground and struggled with it to retrieve his shoes, which were stored under the bed. He carefully manipulated the two heels until they gave way, swinging aside to reveal two small cavities. Inside each cavity was a peach stone. One was made of gold, while at first sight there didn't seem to be anything special about the other.

"As my mother used to say, he who keeps always has," grinned the blind man, revealing two rows of enormous teeth. He took the gold stone and placed it on the palm of his hand. "This is one of Dendria's stones. A premonition made me keep it separate from the rest of the treasure and, as things turned out, it wasn't a bad decision. You must take it with you."

He then took out the peach stone that had a normal appearance.

"Look at this, my friends, because it's something quite extraordinary. This is the stone from the last peach the sacred tree produced before dying. As you can see, it isn't made of gold. Onga and I are unaware of the explanation for this difference, but if there's one thing we're sure about, it's that everything relating to Dendria has a reason. Take it with you, it may help you in your endeavours."

Cecilio placed this last stone next to the gold one and held his hand out to the children. Attica was just about to take them when Onga grabbed her arm to prevent her from doing so.

"Not you, Chiona," she said. "Let the boy take them, let the boy."

The girl looked down, feeling offended, and gave way to Fuco, who stored the two seeds in his already bulky pocket.

"This is the key that gives access to the stairs," announced Cecilio, his trembling hand holding a metal plate in the form of a scorpion with a cylindrical shaft that had been soldered on perpendicularly. Fuco remembered the hole with the exact same shape he'd discovered inside the well and understood it was the lock for this key.

"I could give you a thousand words of advice," continued the blind man, "but unfortunately we don't have much time. The gold stone will lead you to the one who stole the treasure from me."

"How?" asked Attica.

"Don't worry about that, the good-for-nothing will find you himself. When you get the gold back, search for the cornolombrigas. Those creatures are the only way you'll be able to make contact with Dinis and Vinicius."

"And where might we find these corny hamburgers?" asked Fuco.

"Cornolombrigas!" Cecilio corrected him. "Search for a marshy area, that's their preferred habitat. What else?" he pondered. "Avoid main roads, they'll be crawling with Touro's soldiers. After his experience with the two brothers, the Colonel is none too fond of strangers. And try to pass unnoticed, if that's possible... Any questions?"

There were so many doubts they wanted to put into words they ended up dissipating on their lips, preventing them from speaking. Onga got up and took the lamp off its hook. Cecilio started muttering a sort of prayer under his breath, which the children couldn't understand and which he only interrupted to wish them good luck as they left the hut.

The witch accompanied them in a silent walk across the courtyard. When they were standing in front of the wall of the well, Fuco asked her:

"And you, O powerful Onga, Widow of the Darkness, won't you come with us to the land of Nigrofe?"

Onga looked down. Her lips were trembling, and for the first time they detected a hint of fear in her face.

"Remember Arcadia-Lupa, remember," she stammered.

"I know too much, have lived too much... the Green Country could rot my heart."

She turned around and headed for the arch that led away from the tower, while a barn owl started hooting again in the night of the nabrallo.

At the bottom of the well, Fuco placed the key in the hole, and immediately the hexagonal stone moved away to reveal a black hole in the ground.

"You first," he motioned to Attica.

"Coward!" the girl upbraided him, a nervous smile on her lips. She then dropped down into the hole with the lamp, and Fuco followed her. A few seconds later, the slab resealed the entrance. Attica lifted the light. Before them was a steep, spiral staircase.

"Well, here goes!" sighed the girl. And they started their descent■

PART II

NIGROFE

According to data available on 1st July, the population of the city of Audierna is 1,243,840 inhabitants, showing an increase of 160,745 inhabitants with regard to the last census carried out four years ago.

By district, and in order of population,

Linne has .... 328,671 inhabitants,

the Residential Complexes of the North 320,918,

Fundete 247,794,

Seina 242,488

and Plugufan .... 41,199.

The Gwende colonies south of the River Ioke
             have .... 62,770 inhabitants.

There is no official data for the population of the nabrallos. ──────────────────────────

The girls from Seina had some beasts in defence who were really scary. Their technique was about as complex as that of a table, but when it came to dealing out blows, those brutes were unsurpassable! It was on the morning of the last Saturday in September when we came up against them. There had been a frost in the night, the pitch was as hard as a rock. In the changing room, Mrs Kaste, our coach, spent more time warning us to avoid their blows than giving us the necessary instructions on how to win the game. Obviously, we lost, but we received a good beating into the bargain! Even though the game started quite well. In the fifth minute, I scored a goal, which gave us a bonus and put us four points ahead. But, in the move that followed, their left centre-back avenged my affront by tackling me savagely as soon as I received the ball. I ended up face down on the ground, with grazed knees and a dislocated shoulder, as a result of the Seina girl's assault.

That same afternoon, lying on the sofa at home like a queen, I was allowed to ask my family for whatever favours I craved. I was the brave warrior who had returned from the battlefield. Wounded, yes, but worthy of all honour in payment of my sacrifices. My brother, I have to admit, bore the brunt of my whimsical fancies. He was generally a real nuisance, though he could be very sympathetic as well. It was enough for him to see me come home with my arm in a sling for him to turn at once into my most obedient slave.

The day had certainly got off to the worst possible start, but it slowly improved with the passing of the hours. And it did so even more when the doorbell echoed along the walls, forcing my father to leave the kitchen and open the front door.

"Hello, Nivardo! What a surprise, it's been a while!" I heard him say in greeting from the refuge of my sofa. This name froze my blood. What could that clown possibly want?

"Guiomar, guess who's come to see you…"

Nivardo entered the living room and for a moment avoided meeting my gaze. I liked to think his nerves were provoked by a feeling of shame.

"I'll leave you two to it," smiled my father, closing the door.

Neither of us dared to speak. At the third blast of air to remove the flop of hair from in front of his eyes, I had fallen in love with him all over again.

"Are you going to stand there like an idiot?" I asked in the most violent tone I could muster. I folded my legs to make room for him on the sofa. As soon as he sat down, I decided to go on the attack.

"And Deidre?"

He looked down shyly. Normally he was a pretty confident kind of guy, so it was strange to see him like this.

"We split up several days ago," he confessed.

"I had no idea," I said honestly. "I'm very sorry."

Sorry, my foot! I wasn't sorry in the slightest. He told me the witch had a really fiery temper and was always telling him off.

"I feel better like this," he explained very seriously. "You know, more time for my friends and my studies, which I need. How's it going for you at school?"

"Don't ask!" To have said that my marks were poor would have been an understatement, even though we were still a couple of months away from the mid-term exams. Nivardo, on the other hand, as well as being excruciatingly handsome, got the most spectacular marks without even making an effort. It was pretty annoying, that. At least, he wasn't much good at sport. Had he played maila, he would probably have spent more time checking his shirt was clean than paying attention to the match.

We were chatting for about an hour, catching up on what had been happening during those weeks when we were apart. Suddenly, Nivardo got up off the sofa and came over to me, crouching down so he was on a level with my eyes.

"Does it hurt a lot?" He meant my shoulder, though, in my stupefied state, it took me a while to comprehend the question.

"A hell of a lot," I replied seductively.

Our lips drew closer. I could feel his breath on my face when... my brother shot into the room, frightening the life out of us. So much so that Nivardo jumped up and banged his head on the metal lamp hanging from the ceiling.

"Nivardo!" shouted the intruder. "It's great you're here. I've just finished the puzzle of Mount Hodepunke. Do you want to see it?"

"Um... yeah, sure!" he said resignedly, leaving me feeling pretty miffed.

Another good thing about my period of convalescence was being excused from taking notes at school. But my injury prevented me from playing the klavia, which meant my classes came to a temporary halt. To my mother's astonishment, I suggested continuing my visits to the little house on Bagare Street with the false intention of deepening my knowledge of theory. Unfortunately, my stratagem failed.

"You should use those hours to study," said my mother resolutely. "It'll be the mid-term exams soon, and you'll get expelled if you don't do something to improve your marks. You know they don't play about at that school."

She wasn't exaggerating. They were very strict when it came to keeping up your academic level.

But I had bigger things to worry about and – damn it all! – Nivardo had turned into the greatest of them. One sunny Friday towards the end of October, he came over to me in the school playground. Muriel politely moved away, allowing us a moment of intimacy.

"Let's go down to the river," he proposed.

"Are you crazy? What about our lessons?"

He didn't reply. He didn't need to. His smile was enough to persuade me to skip school and accompany him to the bank of the River Ioke.

We sat down on a wooden bench, on the sandy walkway that separates the river from the avenue that runs parallel to it. We could hear the noise of the traffic coming from the road. Opposite, on the other bank, the colonies looked like a huge scale model. We'd been chatting for a while and everything was going swimmingly when suddenly Nivardo did something really stupid.

"Look at those ducks!" he pointed towards the embankment. A family of ducks was floating absent-mindedly on the water.

Nivardo picked up a handful of gravel and tried to hit the ducks with the little stones.

"Hey, leave them alone!" I shouted at him.

Nivardo didn't even answer. He carried on throwing more and more gravel into the water. He had this strange expression on his face, which I judged to be cruel. Perhaps it wasn't. The stones were very small, and the ducks were swimming so far away all he managed was to frighten them. But I was terribly annoyed and started calling him names – animal, idiot, anything I could think of. Perhaps I was momentarily overwhelmed by the rage I felt at the way he'd gone off with Deidre, who knows? The fact is I ended up running away in the same direction as that taken by the Ioke current.

And then a wonderful thing happened: I bumped into Mastrina. It was the first time I'd seen her outside her house. She was walking next to this fat, little man who was dressed in a dark suit with a bowler hat on his head. My teacher was so well wrapped up I found it difficult to recognize her under all those clothes.

She greeted me with a smile and used this opportunity to take her leave of the man with a shake of the hands.

"I swear he's going to drive me crazy!" she exclaimed in a serious voice as the man walked up some concrete steps to the avenue.

"Who is he?" I asked.

"The director of the *Saturn Magazine of Musical Studies*."

"I know that magazine!" Mastrina opened her eyes wide in surprise at my declaration. "My mother's a subscriber!"

"Well, I'm writing a monograph on the evolution of hicupé," she clarified. "I've been slaving away for a month. I've handed in four chapters and devoted a huge amount of time and energy to this project – energy I don't have, by the way. Problems with the contract, they tell me! Were it not for the fact I'm very excited about the whole thing, I'd tell them where to get off!" The old woman pressed the fingers of her gloves against the palms of her hands, making two furious fists. "Ah well! Let's forget all about that sleazeball. Why don't you tell me what you're doing in Plugufan on a Friday morning?"

"I'm not sure I can," I admitted.

"What about school?"

"It was still there when I left it."

She scrutinized me with the clarity of her eyes.

"How's that shoulder of yours?"

"A lot better, I can't complain."

Mastrina took me by the arm.

"Let's walk," she proposed. "Or do you have something better to do?"

"Not at all."

We advanced slowly, in silence, listening to the crunch of our feet on the sand. It was midday, the autumn sun warmed our bodies with a pleasant caress. The benches on the riverbank were occupied by old folk from the district, always under the impenetrable gaze of their Malluma maids.

"So whatever happened to Attica and Fuco?" I asked casually.

Mastrina laughed, resting her head on my healthy shoulder in a gesture of complicity. She then took up the narrative.

"This is awful! My feet are killing me!" complained Fuco.

"Let's rest for a bit," suggested Attica.

They sat down on a step. Attica could feel the cold dampness of the stone on her buttocks. They'd been going down the spiral staircase for such a long time they were dizzy. They'd left Morvane Tower more than an hour earlier, perhaps two. Attica took off her right boot and rubbed her aching foot. The sock was stuck to her skin, and she suspected she had a blister growing on her right toe.

"Did you enjoy the concert?" asked Fuco to alleviate the tension.

Attica had to reorder her thoughts in order to comprehend what he was talking about. How long it seemed since the music of that wonderful quartet, with all those sweaty bodies dancing to its rhythm.

"I loved it, yes," she replied. "They're one of my favourite groups. Amarus Zeno, the klavia player, is an unbelievable talent, I've never seen anyone like him. Do you like hicupé?"

"No," replied Fuco categorically. "I like hic-cup. Hicupé is just a poor imitation."

Attica put her boot back on and pulled on the laces.

"Aren't they the same?"

"Hic-cup is the original version, from Zambela. The people in Bragunde only got wind of it later on," he declared.

"I'd forgotten you were from Zambela."

"I may live in Bragunde, but I was born in Zambela, and all my family's from there."

The girl tied her laces in a rigid knot and picked herself up off the pavement.

"We'd better get a move on."

"That's it, going round in circles!" lamented Fuco. "My brains were almost back where they had to be, so let's stir them up again!"

It wasn't long before they heard a dull noise climbing up the stairwell. Every time they completed a circle, the intensity of the sound got louder until it was this deafening roar that silenced their words.

Fuco tried to say something, but Attica couldn't hear him. Her only response was to urge him with a gesture to keep on going down. Finally, they could make out something different in their descent, a clarity that slowly got brighter as they went around. Their hearts started beating furiously inside their chests.

The staircase came to an end in a cave with a high ceiling, from which hung an inverted army of stalactites. The roar was coming from a powerful waterfall that created this pretty, emerald curtain over what appeared to be the only exit. The verdant gleam splashed about the cave, giving the impression they were in a magical place.

Fuco put his mouth to Attica's ear.

"I was expecting something bigger!" he shouted amid the deafening noise.

"I think you'll find what you were expecting behind the waterfall!"

They were dumbstruck when they set eyes on what was awaiting them behind the water. They were under an infinite, greenish dome from which came a fluorescence that was capable of illuminating a landscape so vast their eyes couldn't take it in. Each and every object was bathed in this light, which seemed to them unreal.

"The Green Country!" exclaimed Fuco, standing there open-mouthed.

In front of them was a forest, which they entered as soon as they were capable of reacting. The trees were all a similar size, none more than two metres high. In some parts, they seemed to have been planted by somebody and stretched out in straight lines. In other places, they were just dotted about haphazardly.

"This must be the Forest of Sanctapersico," reasoned Attica. "We should walk carefully and try not to make any noise."

"Yes, but which way?" asked Fuco, still impressed by the breadth of the landscape.

They walked among the trees, slowly getting used to the new light of Nigrofe.

Suddenly something whizzed over their heads and stuck in the trunk of a tiny pine. It was an arrow.

"To the ground," whispered Attica, dragging Fuco down with her. They lay in the tall grass for a while, then very carefully lifted their heads in search of their aggressor.

From out of the trees, a shadow tiptoed towards them. It was wielding a crossbow, ready for another shot.

It turned out to be a little man with a matted beard and tangled hair tied in plaits. He was wearing a sort of tunic made of fragments of animal skin. Around his neck, he had a very long scarf, also made of skin, like the boots he was wearing and the quiver that hung on his back.

The children ducked down and hid from the crossbowman. As he passed beside them, Fuco leaped up and pulled him to the ground. Attica quickly jumped on top of him, holding one arm against his back and crushing the other with her knee.

"Don't kill me, don't kill me!" pleaded the little man.

"Don't kill you?" exclaimed the girl angrily. "You were the one who almost killed us!"

Fuco picked the crossbow off the ground and aimed it at a tree. He squeezed the trigger, and the weapon spat out an arrow with such devilish force it sent him flying backwards and landed him on his bottom.

"Would you mind not playing the fool and come and help me?" hissed Attica, unable to restrain the man, who kept wriggling about. The boy grabbed his legs, not without getting a few desperate kicks first.

"I swear I wasn't planning to kill you, it wasn't necessary," he implored. "I was out hunting for ratins, just ratins. Please!"

Attica gestured towards Fuco, who picked up the crossbow again and fitted it with a new arrow.

"I'm going to let you go, so no messing around," the girl warned him.

"Thank you, my good lady, thank you!" The man, now free, started kissing her hands. Fuco looked on in amusement.

"Stop with all that nonsense!" Attica pushed him away. "Now, tell us who you are."

"How to explain? I have no name that I know of, it isn't necessary here. I live in the forest and hunt for little ratins, which I feed on. My life is as simple as that."

"Ratins?" inquired Fuco. "What kind of animal is that?"

"Ratins are ratins," declared the man. "The skins I wear come from these animals. There've always been lots of them living in this forest. And yet it's becoming increasingly difficult to find a good specimen. Recently all kinds of intruders have been barging into these woods, soldiers mostly. They pick the fruit and frighten away the ratins, which leave for quieter places. But I'm talking too much, and it isn't necessary."

The man clapped his hand on his mouth, thereby preventing any more words coming out that might cause him a misfortune.

"Don't be afraid," Attica calmed him. "We won't cause you any problems."

Fuco was still fascinated by the subject of ratins.

"If these animals just leave," he said, "then why don't you feed on the fruit? As far as I can see, the trees are laden with it."

"Ah no!" exclaimed the hunter. "That would be a disaster. All the fruit in this forest, without exception, is poisonous. It wouldn't be good to eat – no, it wouldn't."

"Then why do the soldiers pick it?"

"That's a difficult question."

The children judged this frail, distracted-looking man to be inoffensive, so they gave him back his weapon. In gratitude, he invited them to come and have lunch in his house, which he told them was not far away.

They followed him through the trees. The hunter led the way, walking stealthily and peeping out from behind the trunks in search of danger. After a short while, they reached a clearing in the forest, where there was a circular, stone wall about a metre high. The wall had a gap in it, through which the hunter entered, urging the others to follow him.

"Welcome to my house!" declared the man proudly.

"House? It doesn't even have a roof!" retorted Fuco. The man was just about to explain this when the boy took the words out of his mouth: "I know, I know... it isn't necessary."

Fuco set fire to a pine cone, which the hunter placed under some logs until they were blazing. He then skewered three pieces of meat on a long spit and started cooking them over the fire.

"Roast ratin," he informed them. "You'll lick your fingers!"

The children glanced at each other in dismay. The lunch wasn't exactly appetizing. And yet they hadn't eaten in such a long time they finally accepted the invitation. In the end, they even enjoyed the meat, though not so much as the hunter, who gobbled down his helping with unusual voracity.

"These ratins are good!" His mouth and beard were slippery with grease. "Very tender!"

Attica tried to elicit some useful information.

"Does anyone else live in this forest?"

"Recently lots of people have been coming through here, but before that it was always a secluded area."

"Have you always lived here?"

"Where else? I've never known another place. It isn't necessary."

Fuco decided to intervene. He'd finished his piece of meat and quenched his thirst by drinking water from a wineskin that, needless to say, was also made of ratin skin.

"What about your family?" asked the boy, lying on the earthen floor with the wineskin as a pillow.

"I'm not sure I ever had a family. As far as I can recall, I've always been alone."

"But somebody had to teach you how to talk, to hunt, to cook..."

"I suppose so, but I don't remember."

Attica, realizing the conversation was heading nowhere fast, decided to change the subject.

"We're looking for somebody," she confided. "A friend of ours was attacked, and I suspect it wasn't far from here. We want to see his aggressor so we can get back what was stolen from him. Do you know anything?"

The hunter combed his long beard with his fingers, spreading the grease all over the black hair in a glistening film.

"I did hear a struggle," admitted the ratin hunter, "though there wasn't much I could do against that monster."

"Monster?" said Fuco in alarm.

"A huge monster, judging by its shadow. And it wasn't alone, several people were walking alongside it."

Fuco leaned over to Attica and whispered in her ear.

"It seems old Cecilio forgot to mention the small detail of a monster..."

The girl didn't reply. She pursed her lips in a serious gesture and began to think about what she'd heard. Sparks of light shone in the blue of her eyes in front of the bonfire.

"Right, time to sleep," announced the hunter abruptly, interrupting their momentary trance. "You are my guests so you're welcome to sleep here as well if you like."

He untied the scarf around his neck and used it to bandage his eyes. He then lay down on the ground and was soon snoring peacefully.

"It would be a good idea to rest," agreed Attica.

Fuco moved over to the girl, and they both covered themselves with her coat. They were so absolutely exhausted they soon fell fast asleep■

At the end of our walk, we went around Mastrina's house to the garden at the back. A Malluma gardener, who must have been older than the world, was cutting the grass with a machine that made one hell of a racket. Mastrina waved to him, and he replied with this enormous, white smile. We entered the house, and the old woman took off her outer layers in the bedroom.

"Are you staying for lunch?"

"I'd love to, but I can't. I haven't told anybody at home."

She came out of the room and headed to the kitchen.

"When will you be able to continue with the klavia?"

"If all goes well, next Tuesday," I replied from the doorway. "I am going to the doctor on Monday and hope he'll give me the all-clear."

I said goodbye to Mastrina and wandered back through Plugufan in the direction of my district. I thought about Nivardo a little, but not too much, to tell the truth. I had other names on my mind.

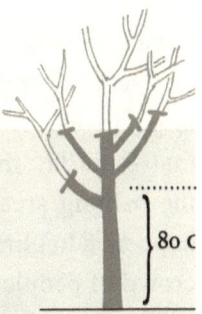
Coincidences can be good or bad, like everything else. The one I'm going to talk about was awful and managed, in a single blow, to ruin my life one foggy Saturday in autumn.

What on earth could have made my personal tutor, Lesmes Rozenne, head over to the Fundete Cultural Association that day, where it so happened my parents were members?

My old man hated visiting the Association's premises and was always supremely bored. They had become members at my mother's insistence and had had to wait a couple of years before being admitted, since the club was one of the most sought-after institutions in the district.

That Saturday, they hadn't even been planning to go, but the cancellation of a lunch date with some friends made a space in their diary that morning, and they decided to fill it by visiting the indoor swimming pool.

The fact is Mr Rozenne's wife had signed up for a course

in painting organized by the Association. At the end of the course, the pupils exhibited their work in the Association's large foyer. The exhibition was due to be inaugurated that Saturday morning and, as my parents were leaving the bathing area, having showered and got dressed, they happened to glimpse my tutor's bald noggin in amongst the crowd of people fighting for canapés.

The day after my walk with Nivardo along the bank of the River Ioke, I had tried to justify my absence from class by claiming a sudden illness. Mr Rozenne, ever on the lookout, asked me for the accompanying doctor's note, which of course I didn't have. I managed to keep him on tenterhooks for a couple of days, until the weekend, in the hope he'd have forgotten all about it, come Monday.

Little did I know that his wife harboured notions of becoming an artist, or that my parents, after all these months, were suddenly going to feel the need to do some exercise on that particular Saturday morning.

The storm that came my way smashed all the records. My mother treated me to her usual bout of hysteria, in which shouts were mixed with sobs of sadness.

But what intimidated me most was my father's sombre face. This usually pleasant and affable man had turned into a stony statue as a result of my truancy.

I tried to pretend it didn't matter so much. Who hasn't skipped a couple of boring lessons on a nice, sunny day? But that was just a new ingredient in my parents' pot, which was already bubbling away on account of my uncertain academic future.

The first measure they took was to ban me from maila. That was non-negotiable. I would rejoin the team after the mid-term exams, so long as I passed every single subject, something that struck me at the time as an implausible dream. But if my expulsion became a reality because of a low percentage in the exams, then the only maila balls I would be seeing in years to come would be the ones on the posters in my room – that is, if they weren't confiscated.

The only positive thing I managed to salvage was my visits to Mastrina and, to achieve this, I had to make use of all my underhand skills.

"I suppose I'm going to have to miss my klavia lessons as well," I sighed to myself.

"Ah no, not that!" roared my mother wildly. "That's what you want. No, you're going to carry on with the klavia, whether you like it or not."

So it was on Tuesday, with my shoulder in perfect conditions, that I turned up on Bagare Street in a reasonably good mood, given the circumstances. I rang several times without getting an answer. The cat with the pink spot came around the side of the house from the path that led to the back garden. It stared at me for a while before retracing its steps and disappearing. I followed it down the path until I glimpsed Mastrina in among the fruit trees. A broad-brimmed, straw hat protected her head from the autumn sun, which was the cause of all kinds of illnesses, according to local folklore. In her hands, covered in rubber gloves, she was holding a knife and a roll of adhesive tape, with which she was busying about a bush. She was so ensconced in her work she didn't notice my presence until I greeted her.

"Good afternoon, Mastrina."

"Guiomar!" she said in surprise. "I wasn't sure you'd be coming today."

I went over to see what she was doing.

"What on earth did this bush do for you to cut it like that?"

"Don't talk rubbish! I'm trying to graft a paarine with a kuepere. It's my third attempt, and I'm hoping this time it'll work."

She used a little knife to make two perpendicular cuts in the kuepere, into which she introduced a paarine shoot. She then joined them together with a piece of tape. As she was completing her task, we heard the trilling of a bird whose shadow I glimpsed in the upper branches of a peach tree.

"There's that ridiculous bird again," complained Mastrina bitterly.

"What's so bad about it, eh? It even has a pretty song."

She didn't reply. She bent back down over the plant and carried on with her task, pressing down the tape with her fingers.

"Don't you have a gardener to do this kind of thing?" I asked.

Mastrina smiled. She looked much better, even the skin on her face was less wrinkled.

"I do it because I like to," she confessed. "Besides, poor Silvano isn't up to this kind of task. He only comes once a week to cut the grass. We've known each other for years, he's been working for my family all his life. It's not easy for me to pay him, given the way things are, but it's a habit I've got into."

She looked up at the sky. Some grey clouds were advancing from the south, bringing the promise of rain.

"We'd better go inside."

I climbed upstairs, that sacred enclosure that contained all the remnants of Mastrina Xaoven's life, in which the klavia, needless to say, occupied pride of place.

I sat on the round stool and listened to her bustling about downstairs. A few minutes later, having freshened up, she climbed the stairs and joined me. She collapsed into her rocking chair.

"What shall we do?" I asked. Mastrina loosened her hair, which formed a white, uniform waterfall that fell down to her shoulders.

"Where were we?" she inquired.

"Attica and Fuco had just gone to sleep in the hunter's house," I reminded her.

She looked at me with a neutral expression that was difficult to decipher.

"I was talking about the klavia. Take that piece of music by Gaëlle. Let's see how rusty your fingers are."

For about an hour, I stuck at this piece, one of few, according to Mastrina, worth rescuing from the corpus of this musician, whom she considered a terrible snob.

When she grew tired of enduring my hesitant interpretation, she sat down next to me and taught me the melody of a beautiful, but slightly sad hicupé. Once I'd got the hang of it, we played at improvising on the theme.

"Do you fancy some tea?" I asked her abruptly. My fingers were starting to ache from so much playing.

"I do," she replied. "And since I know you're not a fan of infusions, you'll find some peach juice in the fridge."

I got up, ready to go down to the kitchen.

"It's a deal," I said from the top of the stairs. "I'll make the drinks, but you start clearing that throat of yours!"

Something disturbed Fuco's rest. In his dozy state, he tried to work out whether it was a nightmare or something sticky and humid really was sliding down his neck. He thought first of all it might have something to do with Attica. The girl might have been playing a trick on him. But when he opened his eyes, he saw it was nothing of the sort. An extremely long, pink tongue was sliding down his chest and introducing its tip into his trouser pocket. It was covered in blisters on the verge of bursting and impregnated with this slimy, transparent spittle. The tongue fiddled about in his pocket until it found what it was looking for. It then rolled itself around the object and began to pull it out. Fuco realized it was stealing the gold stone from Dendria.

He thought about defending himself with his knife, but soon remembered it was in the same pocket as the tongue. Without making any noise, he put his hand in the other pocket. He felt around for the key in the form of a scorpion that Cecilio had given him. He grabbed hold of it and quickly turned around and stuck it in an enormous eye.

The terrifying scream that disturbed the Forest of Sanctapersico also woke Attica and the hunter, who sprang to their feet. Outside the wall of the house, they saw a huge animal crying. The childish sadness of its lament was in stark contrast to its fearful appearance. Thick, black hair covered its whole body, except for its face, which was similar to a human's in terms of the skin and features, but much flatter. It walked on four legs that had four large feet and were arranged in an unusual way, since they grew very close together from the middle of its distended belly. It also had a long, thin tail and some little, rounded ears on top of its head.

There was a short rider on its back, with a crown on his

enormous head and a green parasol in his hand. In the other hand, he was holding a kind of fishing rod, from which hung a gold object. The hunter, as soon as he saw what was going on, greased his shins and legged it into the forest.

"Look what you've gone and done, you damn brutes!" roared the rider before sliding off the monster's back and starting to stroke its face. "There, there, it was nothing..."

But the creature was not to be consoled. The wounded eye looked terrible. Despite being covered by an eyelid, it was obviously very swollen and didn't stop oozing this sticky blood.

Behind the rider and his monstrous mount, in the background, another three men gazed at the scene in astonishment. The similarity between them and the knight was great, though they each had a tuft of orange hair on their head and were still fairly young. They were all wearing black shirts and shorts, their legs swathed in woollen socks that went up to their knees.

"Well, don't just stand there!" shouted the angry man with the parasol. "Give these good-for-nothings a proper hiding!"

The three youngsters didn't budge. They threw the clubs they were carrying on the ground and leaned against the wall with a fastidious air.

"Dad, is it really necessary?" asked one of them nonchalantly.

"Necessary? Look what they've gone and done to my little pet," sobbed the man, hugging the monster's body.

"Your little pet almost tore a leg off a blind man the other day," remarked another of the youngsters.

Their father forgot Fuco and Attica for a moment and turned to confront the rebels.

"We're thieves, assailants, robbers! We steal gold, that's what we do, you bunch of miscreants!"

Fuco took a step forwards and, having bowed very low, addressed the chief of the ruffians.

"Allow me to introduce myself, my lord. My name is Barucus Fuco, son of Dantus Baruc the Firewalker. I am also a robber, like yourself. I am terribly sorry to have wounded your... pet, but it was never my intention to harm a colleague. And yet this must be the result of a terrible misunderstanding. You said you devote yourselves to stealing gold, but we're not carrying any gold at all. May I have the honour of knowing who I am talking to?"

The man gazed at him in distrust. He then walked very stiffly towards the circular wall and bounded up on top of it.

"So, a colleague, eh?" he said scornfully. "Well, it isn't good to lie when among colleagues. My name is Saturn, and I am the finest thief in all of Nigrofe. In my unassailable refuge is kept the greatest treasure you could possibly imagine. My mascot here is a tracker of gold, it brought us here, so there is no doubt you have some gold on you!"

He delivered the last part of this sentence in a roaring voice, his face livid with rage. Attica opted to intervene.

"Might it have been tracking this?" she pointed at her nose, which had a gold ring in it.

Saturn's sons leaned forward to see the girl.

"All this because of some piddling ring?" said one of them.

"It seems things are going from bad to worse..." lamented another.

"I'm going home," declared the third before turning around and moving off silently among the trees.

"Come back here, you cowards, you twits!" exclaimed Saturn, beside himself with rage. "This is an utter disaster..."

The monster tracker snivelled and affectionately rubbed

its head against Saturn's chubby legs. Saturn disconsolately stroked its head. Fuco went over, causing the monster to back away in fear.

"There may be a way I can make up for this misfortune," he declared.

These words piqued the robber's curiosity, and he leaned over to hear what the boy had to say.

"Go on."

"Well, it's very simple. Since we're both robbers and you boast about the impregnability of your hiding place, I bet you whatever you like that I'm capable of entering the place where you keep your booty and stealing something."

Saturn, who'd been listening with his eyes open wide, emitted an enormous guffaw that alarmed the monster even more.

"Do you know what it is you're saying, my dear?" he mocked him. "You wouldn't be able to find the place where I keep my treasure, let alone enter it, even if you had a whole year."

"I only need a couple of hours," said Fuco resolutely. "Accept the bet then, if you're so sure I'll fail."

The man sat down on the stones and scratched his head.

"What are we betting?"

"If I can do it, you let me take whatever I like from your treasure. If not, you take whatever you want from us."

Saturn looked the two children up and down. They didn't have much to offer, that was obvious. Attica's nose ring, the most valuable object the thief had seen, was insignificant in comparison with his own sumptuous treasure.

"I know what I want," he said finally. "My sons, poor things, you've seen what they're like. They're not exactly what I would call go-getters. I'd always doubted they would get married and, when Touro shut all the women up in Venquinta, well, I lost the little hope I had. Besides, as the days go by, they seem less and less interested, and I'm getting old. If I win the bet, this blond-haired girl will marry one of them. She looks healthy enough and can give me some strong grandchildren to carry on the business."

Attica smiled at this proposal and was just about to give the man a scolding when Fuco spoke.

"I agree."

The girl stared at him with her eyes on stalks.

"Are you crazy?" she hissed, grabbing hold of his sleeve. The boy's pleading look, however, persuaded her to trust him.

"We agree," confirmed Fuco.

"Very good, very good..." sniggered Saturn before climbing back on to the beast. "I'll be back in a couple of hours to receive my payment."

The monster, whose eye had stopped bleeding, turned and galloped off among the trees. Saturn guided it by moving the gold object hanging from the fishing rod. Surprisingly, given its enormous size, it was as silent as a kitten.

"I take it we have a plan," said Attica in concern.

"That's right," Fuco calmed her down. "Now let's sleep. We've a couple of hours to rest a little."

The boy lay back down with his head on the wineskin. He covered himself with the coat and was soon sleeping peacefully. Attica, on the other hand, knowing she wasn't going to get a wink, sat on the stone wall and prepared to wait. Looking through the leaves, she discovered some eyes watching her.

"You can come out now," she said to the hunter.

The man climbed down from a cherry tree and entered the house, still afraid.

"Is everything OK?" he asked.

"We'll soon find out," replied the girl.

Just as he'd promised, two hours later, Saturn returned to the clearing, followed by his offspring. He was again riding the monster tracker, whose wounded eye was covered in a bulky bandage. Attica woke Fuco with a little kick, and the boy stretched his limbs, which were still numb from sleeping.

"So?"

Fuco stood in front of him. Despite the difference in age, they were about the same height.

"I believe you've lost the bet," said the boy boldly, a broad smile spreading across his face.

The man started laughing hysterically. He looked at his sons in search of their complicity, but they just looked back at him with bored expressions.

"Show me then," he asked when he'd finally grown tired of laughing.

Fuco put his hand in his pocket and took it out with the fist clenched, which he opened slowly in front of Saturn. On his palm, the gold stone Cecilio had given him shone in the greenish light of Nigrofe.

"No way!" exclaimed Saturn in astonishment, his features distorted. "That's impossible!"

"There was a whole pile of stones, though I think one is sufficient proof, don't you?"

"It's a trick, a vile stratagem! My treasure is unassailable!"

Fuco placed the gold object in front of his eyes.

"Are you sure?"

Saturn didn't reply. He simply left the house and got back on the monster.

"This stone is your only reward," he said to Fuco. "Keep it. I'm not giving you any more."

Attica jumped over the wall and grabbed the man by one leg, pulling him to the ground.

"You're going to stick to the terms of our agreement, you conniving knave!" she threatened him, raising her fist to his face. Attica's move provoked a reaction in the monster, which came to its master's aid. Roaring fiercely, it opened its jaws, revealing two lines of jagged teeth, which it would have stuck in the girl's back had it not been for the decisive action taken by Saturn's children.

"Quieten down, you lot!" shouted one of them, placing himself between the opponents. Attica let go of Saturn, who stood up with a red face and shook the dust off his clothes. His son addressed him, "Dad, we're thieves, not liars, so you must keep your word."

"But that's impossible..."

"Dad!"

"OK, OK..." mumbled the robber before turning to Fuco. "What is it you want?"

"The other gold stones," declared the boy confidently.

"Is that all?"

"That will be sufficient."

"You'll have them here in less than an hour," agreed Saturn, getting back on the monster tracker. He then left the clearing, followed by his offspring.

Attica went over to Fuco and placed a hand on his shoulder.

"Well played," she said.

"You weren't too bad yourself, Chiona," laughed the boy. "Though we need to work out who's the brains and who's the brawn in this partnership■"

150

TREGÜEILE ON ROLANDE'S INFIDELITY

"I THOUGHT I'D FALLEN OFF A SKYSCRAPER"

The ex-first lady of Audierna denied she was going through a crisis, since it isn't the first break-up in her life, "though it is the most upsetting because of all the repercussion in the media." The woman who was the President of the Confederation's partner in recent years, Vanora Tregüeile, said that finding out about Faxildo Rolande's relationship with the soprano Gavenia Xaoven was like falling off a skyscraper, though she had been aware of the rumours.

"Obviously I'd heard the rumours, but you hear them all the time, about everybody – including me! I didn't pay them any attention. When I found out, it was like falling off a skyscraper," declared Tregüeile.

It always happens like this, there's no getting around it. Sunny days are made to coincide with periods of confinement. The clever weather must have known all about my punishment because, to everybody's surprise, the first weeks of the month of November brought not only clear skies, but also pleasant temperatures that made you want to go out in the street.

I'm not going to talk anymore about Nivardo, enough said. We argued and became friends so many times during those days it would be dull in the extreme to record all our struggles here.

So I shall try to concentrate on my relationship with Mastrina Xaoven, the heart of the story I wish to tell.

The following Thursday, I turned up on time for my appointment in the old district of Plugufan. On entering Mastrina's house, I noticed the succulent smell of roast meat coming from the kitchen. To this unusual circumstance must be added the fact my teacher was dressed very elegantly, something I had never seen since starting my lessons. She was wearing a black skirt to below the knee, a high-necked, red jersey and some shoes, also black, in place of her customary flannel slippers. As if this weren't enough, she had tied her hair in a bun and put some rouge on her cheeks.

"Wow, Mastrina! You look wonderful. Are you expecting somebody?"

"I'm expecting you," she answered, a little embarrassed. We went upstairs.

In the klavia room, she told me she had a dinner date, so our meeting, unfortunately for me, would be limited to an hour and a half in front of this instrument that, to tell the truth, I was starting to hate a little less.

It was when we said goodbye that something quite unusual happened. As I was going around the corner of the ironmonger's, I almost bumped into a man. He was quite good-looking for his age, with small eyes behind round glasses and thick, white hair parted at the side. He was wearing a grey suit with a red bow tie and carrying a parcel wrapped up as a present in his hands. The man apologized profusely and headed towards Mastrina's door.

I know it's not good to spy on people, but this happened so long ago time itself has probably absolved me of my curiosity. Peeping around the corner, I watched the scene unfold. Mastrina opened and threw herself into the arms of this stranger, who kissed her on the cheek. It was then, amid all the murmurings of the evening in that old quarter, that I heard a greeting that pummelled my brains over the next few days: "Good evening, Attica. How are you?"

These words banged and clattered about inside my head the whole weekend. The days and hours just wouldn't go by. They slunk slowly and stickily across the clock, like a drop of honey on a glass surface.

The following Tuesday, I waited for the bell that signalled the end of classes with particular unease. If it was usually difficult for me to concentrate at school, that day I couldn't register a single word my teachers said.

When the bell finally resounded down the corridor, waking the classes from a day of boredom, an uncontrollable flood of pupils poured out the door and on to the street. I was the tip of the arrow and left the other children behind, running between those proud houses with their front gardens. I turned on to 15 August Avenue in the direction of Plugufan and didn't stop running until I was in the shade of the old oak.

"Good afternoon, Guiomar. Is someone chasing you?"

I obviously wasn't in the mood for any preambles.

"Tell me something, what is your name?"

Mastrina knew what I was thinking and avoided my inquisitorial gaze.

"Come upstairs. I was just looking at some old photos."

I followed her to the klavia room. Lying on the floor, next to the curved supports of the rocking chair, a cardboard box full of ancient photographs was waiting for us. Mastrina gestured to me to pull up the round stool and sit down next to her.

"Your name's Attica," I blurted, searching out her eyes. "Or at least that's what your guest called you."

"Were you never taught that it's rude to spy on people?"

"Why beat about the bush?"

"Yes, my name is Attica. It's a common enough name."

"Sure it is! I don't know anyone by the name of Attica – except you. And that leads me to ask myself a whole succession of questions."

"Well, you shouldn't, I've already told you how things are. Attica, Guiomar, Elba… they're just names, useful when it comes to narrating situations. If there are gaps in my imagination that need filling, why shouldn't I lay hold of what's familiar?"

I involuntarily rubbed my hands against my skirt, a gesture I make when I'm thinking. I also looked for the cats. They weren't anywhere to be seen. Perhaps they hadn't come home yet and were making the most of this unexpected let-up in the weather. Mastrina continued going through the old photos.

"And the man with the bow tie?" I asked.

Without saying anything, she rummaged inside the box and pulled out a black-and-white photograph, which she handed to me. In it, a boy and a girl were seated on two swings and smiling at the lens. Mastrina's house served as a backdrop, together with part of the back garden. The swings and rosebushes in the photograph, like symbols of a happier past, had disappeared with the years.

"He's my twin brother," explained my teacher. "He's also the one in the photograph you knocked over on your first visit."

I carried on gazing at this portrait of the two siblings. They were very little. How many years had passed since then? Sixty perhaps, or more…

Mastrina kept handing me photographs, images from the past showing unfamiliar faces, unusual hairstyles and old-fashioned clothes.

"Does he often come to visit you?" I asked.

She smiled bitterly at this question, without taking her eyes off the past.

"Not as often as we'd both like," she confessed. She seemed to want to share this burden with me. "He lives in the north, in a small town where he worked as a teacher. He came to give me some money. The treatment of this disease has left my housekeeping in ruins. My dear brother was always better at saving! He inherited my mother's money; I, on the other hand, got her illness and this house, another of her whims. When she bought it, it was in the centre of the main district in Audierna. Now, it isn't worth a thing. Here's my mother. She's beautiful, isn't she? She was a wonderful soprano…"

She certainly was very attractive. She had this incisive look that transmitted a sense of unease, as if she were shouting at me with her eyes. I felt obliged to put the photograph back in the box.

"What about your father?"

"We never knew him. My mother… how should I put it? She had this unusual character. She was normally a sweet and affectionate woman, but when a gust of wind hit her weathervane, it was better to get out of the way!" Mastrina laughed nostalgically. "I'd heard rumours and one day I resolved to ask about him. Well, would you believe it? She started screaming her head off. 'He's dead, dead and buried!' Obviously, I never brought the subject up again. Even though I was always the brave one – a rebel, if you like. My brother… well, he's much more docile. They were very close. He suffered terribly during the final phase of her illness, which is why he never asks how my own illness is progressing. He behaves like an ostrich. He helps in any way he can without hesitating, but when it comes to the question of my health, he's utterly blind, or at least that's the impression he gives."

She glanced at her watch.

"It's getting late," she remarked.

"Mastrina, I don't feel like playing today. I say this quite openly. You're always talking about having love for your instrument and all that. Well, I couldn't say I love it quite yet, but I am acquiring a degree of fondness for the thing. That said, there are days when I need my own space, you know what it's like… And I don't want this burgeoning relationship between us to die from overexposure…"

"You're a crafty one, you are," remarked the old woman without a hint of anger in her voice. "It's getting cold. You'd better go and fetch those blankets from the wardrobe."

They filled up a water bottle the hunter had given them – needless to say, it was made of ratin skin. The man, who was totally unused to having dealings with other humans, enjoyed these last few moments in the company of the children as much as possible. He was so excited he decided to present the boy with a skin jacket.

"Nigrofe's roof has several mouths," he explained. "When the mouth Arcta belches, an icy gust crosses the country from north to south. You can't go moseying around without a good coat."

A short while later, Saturn's sons turned up with their black clothes and carrot-coloured tufts. One of them was carrying a little bag, which he opened in front of the children to reveal the contents. It was full of gold stones, just as Saturn had promised. Fuco took out the gold stone Cecilio had given him and put it with the others in the bag. The second stone – the last seed Dendria had produced with its normal appearance – he preferred to keep hidden away in his pocket.

"That's great!" said Attica. "Now we'd better get going."

"Where are you headed?" asked one of the thief's sons.

"That's right, Attica, where are we headed?" remarked Fuco quizzically.

The girl gave him a withering look, annoyed at what he'd said. She didn't want these youngsters finding out they had no fixed direction. Attica cast about for some useful information.

"We're looking for a marshy area."

The brothers gazed at each other in consternation.

"What for?" asked one of them, who had this pink spot on his nose that singled him out from the rest.

"It's just that we like mud and nasty smells," Fuco endeavoured to help her.

"We're looking for the cornolombrigas," the girl finally admitted.

Attica took the bag and made for the exit of the hunter's house. The voice of one of the brothers stopped her in her tracks.

"Can we go with you?"

"With us? Are you looking for a marsh as well?"

"No, we're going to Venquinta, and there's a marsh along the way. But no cornolombrigas have been seen there for quite some time."

"So you're abandoning old Saturn and his pet dog..." observed Fuco.

"We're tired of living purely for the sake of accumulating gold. We have other pretensions. I, for one, would like to open a tavern in Venquinta Town."

A second brother came up to Attica and whispered surreptitiously in her ear:

"And I'm going to join the resistance against Touro."

All looks were then aimed at the brother with the spot on his nose, who had yet to reveal his reason for not wanting to be a ruffian anymore.

"I just can't put up with Dad," he explained. "If you're all leaving, I'm not staying with him for all the gold in the world."

Saturn's sons introduced themselves as Xes, Zeno and Prisco. They then led the children through the Forest of Sanctapersico until the trees abruptly gave way to a broad landscape of rolling hills. The ground was covered in thick, short grass. Their emergence from the forest coincided with the reappearance of the scorpions. Their numbers increased the further away the walkers got from the trees. First, there was just the odd one scuttling about in the grass. Then they saw little groups which, a short while later, turned into lengthy lines that crawled across the ground. Despite wearing sturdy boots, Saturn's sons walked close together, each carrying a stick with which to ward off the insects. And yet, for some strange reason, the arachnids fled in terror at the sight of the travellers and didn't bother them at all.

The group followed a sandy path that broke the uniformity of the grass. The sky – or rather, the ceiling – was a permanent, unending, greenish glint in the heights.

From time to time, a wall encircled a field, something that struck them as pointless – since leaving the forest, they hadn't seen any cattle at all.

They climbed along a succession of closed curves up the side of a hill. A stream ran downhill, in its hasty descent creating small waterfalls whose rustling sound kept the travellers company. Between the stream and the path was a steep meadow surrounded by a barbed-wire fence. In the middle of this meadow, motionless as a statue, they saw an enormous bird. Its feathers were yellow, except on the wings, where they were blue. It had a bright red crest and two sharp spurs on the back of its feet. It stood with its head raised and its beak open, as if it were singing. And yet no sound came out of its mouth.

"Well, blow me down!" exclaimed Fuco, going up to the fence. "What kind of bird is that?"

Prisco, the brother with the spot on his nose, left the path and went to join him. Every now and then, he glanced at the ground, searching for possible dangers in the grass.

"Strange animals, the flavacocos," he said. "They spend the whole day standing still – except, that is, when they're hungry..."

"I have to see this thing up close!" Fuco interrupted him, slipping through the barbed wire and running towards the exotic bird.

"... or when they feel threatened," said Prisco, finishing his sentence when there was no one to hear him.

Fuco ran across the wet grass of the field. At this point, to his surprise, it started raining. Drops as fat as apples fell slowly and constantly from the ceiling. It was nothing like the rain up on the surface.

On reaching the flavacoco, the boy calculated it must have been about two metres tall. A gentle breeze ruffled its yellow feathers. Fuco gazed at his companions, who were all waving at him and making strange gestures. Attica had climbed one of the fence posts and was urging him to return to the path.

"Who's the coward now?" muttered the boy to himself.

He slowly raised his hand to the bird's chest. He felt short of breath, though his own heart was beating away furiously. He had just softly caressed one of the feathers with his fingertip when he heard this enormous roar that almost deafened him. The flavacoco gave a little jump and knocked him over with a kick to the chest, which left him lying stunned on the ground. He recovered from the blow just in time to dodge a violent stamp, which, had it reached its target, would have crushed his skull. He tried to get to his feet and start running, but a second blow knocked him over again. He did a clever somersault and managed to run towards the fence, where his friends were shouting in despair. The bird's heavy footsteps pounded along behind him.

The boy then saw something that frightened him almost as much as his angry pursuer. Inside the field, only a couple of metres away, a little man was walking towards them. His face was covered in a white mask that had an unsettling appearance and shadowy features, a prominent nose in the shape of a bird's beak and two eyes made of red crystals. The rest of his body was hidden by a thick, black coat, the tails of which dragged along the ground, and on his head he wore a broad-brimmed hat. He walked with these strange, little steps, leaning on a stick that was far bigger than he was.

Fuco managed to reach the fence and slip through the barbed wire to safety. From there, he saw how the man stopped in front of the flavacoco, which came to a halt and started pawing at the grass with its feet while roaring ferociously.

The man in the mask raised his stick and uttered some words in an unfamiliar language. Immediately, all the scorpions in the area headed towards the bird, first surrounding it and then climbing its body until it was fully covered. The flavacoco went into violent convulsions, trying to shake off the blanket of insects. All in vain. When it opened its beak to complain of the pain caused by the stings of dozens of scorpions, the scorpions scuttled inside its throat, silencing it and then causing its death.

The man in the mask went over to the group, which had been watching the scene inside the field in astonishment. Saturn's sons prostrated themselves in front of him out of respect. Attica and Fuco, who knew nothing about what was going on, remained standing.

"Are you crazy?" hissed Zeno from the ground. "Prostrate yourselves before him, it's the Bird Man."

The two children, overwhelmed by the confusing situation, made as if to bow. A voice then resounded from inside the mask.

"Stay on your feet, travellers. It isn't necessary to show any sign of respect."

Attica and Fuco stood up straight. The three brothers, however, chose to ignore these words and continued lying motionless on the ground.

"Tell me, where does your path lead?" asked the Bird Man.

Attica weighed up the virtues of telling him the truth. She glanced at the bag with the gold stones.

"We're looking for a marsh," she replied simply.

The Bird Man took a step forwards. Fuco thought he saw a malignant gleam behind the red crystals of his eyes.

"In which case, our paths coincide. I have visited more than half the marshes in Nigrofe, worried as I am about the disappearance of the cornolombrigas."

When she heard this last sentence, Attica opened her eyes wide.

"Do you have any idea how to find them?"

"Only rumours, really. Why? Are you also looking for the messengers of the earth?"

Fuco shook his head, while Attica nodded enthusiastically.

"Well, I think if we join forces, we might be able to find them more quickly."

Fuco tugged on the sleeve of Attica's coat and led her to one side.

"Have you gone crazy?" he hissed in her ear. "Are you going to trust this guy? What if he's just another thief who wants to steal our gold?"

"Our gold? You're the crazy one. That gold isn't ours. We have to find Dinis and Vinicius and give them the bag. And that's why we have to find the cornolombrigas as soon as we can."

"Well, let's try to find them ourselves. That old scarecrow gives me the willies."

"Are we going to reject the only lead we have, just because

it gives you the willies? You might have let that bird give you the willies – you almost went and got yourself killed for playing the fool."

"I'd already escaped from the bird. It wasn't necessary to kill it."

Attica turned her back on the boy in a huff. She grabbed the bag from the ground and headed towards the fence. On the other side, the Bird Man was waiting.

"We're coming with you," she declared.

The man climbed through the barbed-wire fence. He was wearing black, leather boots that ran under the tails of his coat and seemed to go on forever. At every step he took, the scorpions retreated out of respect, or perhaps out of fear.

"Let's go then," said the voice behind the mask, which was neutral and mysterious, before starting to walk with Attica following behind.

Saturn's sons remained in their position, lying on the grass.

"I'm not going!" declared Fuco firmly.

The Bird Man ignored his words and continued along the path, leaning on his stick. Attica, however, came to a halt and stared at Fuco.

"What's that? Stop messing around."

"You can go if you like, I'm staying with these boys. We had a plan, and I'm going to stick to it."

"What about the bag?"

"I'll think of something."

Blind with rage, Attica abandoned her friend and ran after the Bird Man. It wouldn't take her long to regret this decision∎

Lack of Light

If a plant spends too much time without sun, it will stop producing flowers and eventually die. Existing flowers will wither and turn brown or black. The time it can spend without light before its flowers start withering depends on the plant, some species being more resistant than others. A large plant can generally spend more time without sun, up to a couple of months, before it dies. But its flowers will die in a matter of days so as to conserve energy. Smaller plants can only survive a couple of days before their flowers wilt and die shortly before the plant does. Some, like the "resurrection plant," a kind of *Selaginella*, can live several years without sun, reducing their metabolic processes to a minimum.

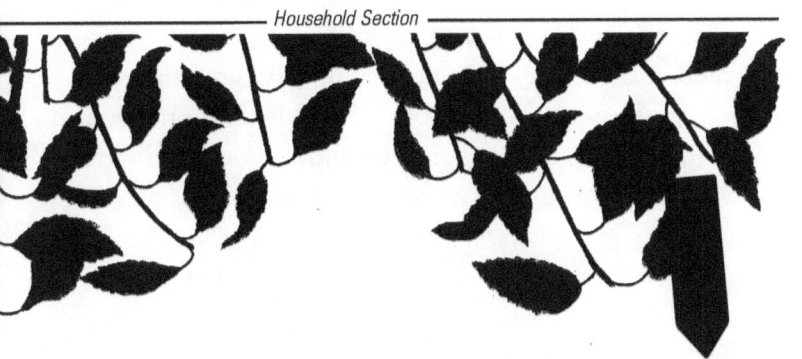

Thursday finally brought some good news: Mr Rozenne – also known as *Merry Donkey,* a nickname inherited from previous generations of students – was ill. This meant our last lesson in the afternoon was cancelled. Muriel and a group of girls from my class decided to use this unexpected leisure time to visit the recreational facilities on the North Ring. I declined the invitation to go with them and brought forward my visit to the old quarter.

"You're becoming very antisocial, Guiomar," Muriel rebuked me, and she may have been right. "What on earth makes you want to spend so much time in that old biddy's house? I remember when you were spitting fire just because your parents wanted to make you go."

What answer could I give her? Obviously, not the truth. If she was mildly annoyed with me now, I didn't want to think what she'd say if she discovered the reason for my absence was a story. A children's story, perhaps, though for me it was a hundred times more exciting than the teenage novels of Luan Briegue, which were all the rage in the schools of Audierna at that time.

Some minds are more open to fantasy, while others are more earthbound. "Magic cannot hide on palates of stone," in the words of the poet. Muriel had no problems entering the bodies of languid, romantic heroes who were as transcendental as the breath of death, but I couldn't imagine her in Attica's shoes, buried alive in a tomb or facing up to a monster in the legendary Green Country.

At Mastrina's house, there was no answer when I rang on the doorbell, so I thumped on the door with my fists and got the same result. I peeped through the curtains on the ground floor and only came across one of the cats sleeping placidly on the bedroom windowsill.

I had arrived an hour before my lesson was due to start. Probably, I thought, Mastrina had gone out on an errand and would be back soon.

The doors were locked, so I decided to wait in the garden. I meant to sit under one of the fruit trees, but the autumn sun, which barely reached the back of the house, had yet to dry the grass, which was still damp from the previous night's frost.

I ended up sitting on a wooden bench on its own in front of the hedge that protected the neighbouring property's privacy.

I rummaged about in my rucksack for my book of modern literature. I decided to use this time to study a little. And yet the subject matter was so dull it made me feel very drowsy. The soft light of autumn and the chirping of the birds combined to gently rock me to sleep.

I was woken by somebody tickling my nose with a blade of grass. When I opened my eyes, I found two faces gazing at me.

"Tell me you're not skipping class again," demanded Mastrina.

Next to her was a woman in her fifties with short hair and small eyes with swollen bags beneath them. She was pretty and had a pleasant expression, a white smile and freckly cheeks.

I felt embarrassed and used the sleeve of my coat to wipe away the dribble coming from the corner of my mouth.

"The teacher didn't turn up, I swear," I said in self-defence.

The two women were carrying large shopping bags. I got up from the bench, and Mastrina introduced me to her companion.

"This is Dr Dame Kirdegarde, probably the best Volbloede specialist in all of Audierna."

"Stop exaggerating, Attica!" the doctor went red. "There are far better doctors than me."

"Don't be so modest! Now let's go inside."

I followed the women into the house. In the kitchen, they placed the bags on top of the table. Dr Kirdegarde then refused an invitation to tea, saying she had a prior engagement.

"I arranged to pick my daughter up in Verrenorde so we could go to the theatre, and I'm already late. But next time I promise to stay for a chat."

She took her leave of her friend with two kisses on the cheek and of me with a shake of the hands.

When she'd gone, Mastrina took the products out of the bags and started distributing them in the cupboards. I offered to help her, but she turned me down, saying I didn't know where anything went.

"It's already half past," I declared, making known my intentions.

Mastrina pretended not to hear me and staggered on to a chair to reach the upper shelves of a cupboard. I went over to steady her, and this time she accepted my help.

"Shall we use this half hour before the lesson?" I insisted.

Mastrina gently stroked my hair from her superior position.

"Let me just put all this away, and we'll start."

In Nigrofe, there was neither night nor day. The green light projected by that unknown mineral that made up the dome was continuous and eternal. And yet there were places where a thick mist rose from the ground, its ethereal, chalk fingers poking in and out of nooks and crannies.

Along the way, Saturn's sons and Fuco avoided the main roads so they wouldn't bump into any of Colonel Touro's troops. With the passage of time, the landscape had changed completely, and what had once been rolling hills coated in grass had given way to a rough, uneven territory of pointed rocks and paths bordering deep gullies. There was scant vegetation, just the odd, solitary bush.

The legions of scorpions continued parading past along the narrow tracks, but timidly avoided the wayfarers.

"Look at those bugs," said Prisco to Fuco. "They're heading to Venquinta, just like us. We couldn't have chosen a worse moment to undertake this journey."

"You can still go back," replied Fuco.

"Go back to my Dad with my head down? I'd rather sleep on a mattress of scorpions."

Zeno, the bravest of the brothers, left the path and clambered up a rock until he was lost in the mist.

"Come up here!" he shouted from the heights.

The other three followed in his footsteps, climbing the rock until they reached a completely level platform. Zeno welcomed them enthusiastically.

"Look at this!" he cried. "A perfect hiding place. We can rest here for a while."

They managed to gather a few dry sticks from the mountainside, which they piled in the middle of the stone platform. Fuco set fire to them with his lighter, and they all sat around the flames. They were exhausted.

Xes, the future tavern-keeper, took some enormous, white sausages out of his rucksack and skewered them on a spit to roast them over the fire.

Fuco stayed a little way off from the rest of the group. He was tired and beset by fear and sadness. Prisco went over to offer him a sausage.

"I don't suppose it's ratin?" joked Fuco bitterly.

"Yes, how did you know?"

Although his stomach was as shrivelled as an empty wineskin, Fuco did all he could to ingest the food, which he washed down with an occasional sip from his bottle. He thought about Attica, who'd left without any water. Stubborn Chiona!

"Tell me about the Bird Man," said the boy.

This request surprised Prisco, who was combing the curly hair in his tuft.

"I'd heard about him when I was little, but that's the first time I've ever seen him," he began. "You're not from around here, are you? You and the girl. All the women in Nigrofe have been shut up in Venquinta for quite some time."

169

"We've come... from far away," stuttered Fuco, unable to find the right words.

Prisco stared at him in silence. The flames danced erratically over his face, the wood crackling away in the background. The green light of Nigrofe was obscured by drops of mist, which added to the confusion of the dancing shadows. Saturn's son went on with his explanation.

"According to the legend, there is another world beyond our own frontiers, a world we used to be at one with. One day, our people were struck by a terrible disease. Those were the days of Puna. Entire families died, touched by the finger of misfortune. Corpses piled up in the squares and streets, and nobody knew how to bring this implacable punishment to an end. The government at the time opted for a radical solution: all those who had contracted the disease, and those who had come into contact with them, would be transferred to Nigrofe, the outer world being reserved for healthy people. Then the gates of the Green Country would be shut and hidden, thus burying the cruel disease■"

"I've heard that story!" My shout startled Mastrina, who was talking from the balcony. I'd taken her place in the rocking chair, swinging rhythmically while listening to her story. "Artusa used to tell it to me before I went to sleep."

"It's a well-known Malluma legend," replied the old woman. "Now may I go on?"

"Yes, please."

Prisco went on with his story.

"A young man, who was still training to be a healer, worked with the sick in Nigrofe. He came from a good family and, despite his parents' pleas, refused to go back home, so he was buried along with his patients. He was convinced he could stop Puna and would put his own life at risk if necessary to prove this. The people, who were petrified, gathered around the walls of Venquinta Monastery, which at that time rose on top of a hill in the centre of a large plain, since the town had yet to be built. The healer wore a long coat, high boots, gloves, a broad-brimmed hat and a mask in the form of a bird's beak. Inside the beak, he placed a mixture of herbs and seeds to filter the bad air and protect himself from possible infection. Among those who were trapped in Nigrofe, he became known as the Bird Man – they didn't know his real name, and nobody had ever seen his face. The healer attended people one by one. He told them to get undressed and burned their clothes. He then bathed them in water, vinegar and garlic, and ordered them to drink a potion he prepared in large cauldrons.

"The epidemic gradually declined, but the vast amount of healing left him feeling exhausted. When he'd finished his work, he withdrew to the Grove of Coenobio to rest and disappeared for several centuries."

Prisco clicked his fingers to emphasize this last sentence. Fuco coughed to clear his throat.

"He disappeared?" he asked.

"Yes, he vanished completely. This mysterious disappearance served only to increase his legendary status. After that, the Bird Man was venerated in Nigrofe like a kind of saint, a mystical being, something that never went down too well inside the monastery, where this devotion was seen as an obscene, pagan gesture."

Prisco dragged his bottom over the grey stone to inch closer to Fuco.

"And yet, some years ago, the Bird Man reappeared. Ever since then, he's been wandering the paths of Nigrofe, behaving in a cruel way that has nothing to do with the kind, altruistic man of the legend. Even in the Forest of Sanctapersico, always so far removed from the rest of the country, there have been reports of his cruelty. What is more, it's said he has become Colonel Touro's adviser, in his presence the colonel is nothing more than a Jack-under-the-bed and it was his idea to shut up all the women in the monastery."

Although he kept trying to dodge these thoughts, remorse had been acting on Fuco ever since they'd separated from Attica. Prisco's words added a few more stones to his bag of repentance.

At this point, Attica was struggling over a cracked wasteland. Not even a scrawny plant grew in that desert, which was sown with the skeletons of animals that had been unfortunate enough to wander into those lands. Thousands of scorpions marched in organized lines that seemed to go on forever. Tiredness had laid hold of her legs, she could feel her body getting heavier with every step she took. It was impossible to work out how many hours she'd been walking alongside the Bird Man, who, despite his uncomfortable attire, didn't show any signs of weakening and kept up a lively pace by banging his stick on the ground.

To the cramp in her legs was added the dryness in her mouth, the bitter taste of the foul, clammy air in that wasteland having settled on her palate.

Attica noticed a couple of black dots buzzing about the horizon. These dots slowly grew and took on the appearance of two soldiers who were walking sluggishly along and leaning on their spears. They wore brown, leather armour, round helmets crowned by white tufts and long, stained, white capes.

Just as Saturn's sons had done before them, the soldiers prostrated themselves on the ground and lay motionless when they became aware of the Bird Man's presence. Attica used this opportunity to grab one of their water bottles and quench her thirst. She would have drunk all the water had she not felt sorry for the pitiful state they were in.

The Bird Man, who had ignored the soldiers and carried on walking, stopped some yards ahead and silently observed Attica's gesture.

"I'm sorry, new friend, I hadn't realized you were tired," he said when the girl came up alongside him. "Would you like to rest a bit?"

"That would be nice," said Attica imploringly, sitting down on the cracked earth. She glanced at the soldiers, who were now covered by dozens of lively scorpions that had moved out of line. "Please tell them to get up."

The Bird Man fixed her with his disturbing, red stare before speaking.

"If that's your wish, you can tell them yourself."

The girl went over to the soldiers and informed them that they were allowed to get up. They had several swollen bites on their legs, which they treated by covering them in poultices they had brought along for this purpose in their rucksacks. They then got up very slowly, never turning their backs on the others and bowing constantly.

Attica returned to where the Bird Man was. The scorpions moved aside, creating a circle around them that was several metres in diameter.

"You can sit over there, they won't bother you at all," said the voice behind the mask. "My brothers and sisters would never hurt you in my presence."

Attica collapsed on the ground and took off her boots to find out the lamentable state her feet were in – much to her dismay.

Her companion, however, remained standing, erect like a horrifying scarecrow in the middle of nowhere.

"Tell me, new friend, why are you searching for the cornolombrigas?" he asked abruptly.

"I have a present for them," said the girl, having thought for a moment. She knew that what she'd said was really dumb, but it was the best answer she could come up with.

"What is it you might have to give to the cornolombrigas? Those repulsive beings are just messengers, their nature forbids them to accept any presents."

Attica made a false attempt at smiling to lower the tension. She felt trapped. But something then happened to divert her interrogator's attention. A white scorpion came to the edge of the protective circle. It was at least three times as big as its fellows. It stood up on its hind legs and waited respectfully for the Bird Man to approach its position. The mask spoke to it in that strange language it had already used during the episode with the flavacoco and fell silent to listen to the scorpion's inaudible answer. It then raised its stick in a rage and strode off in the same direction they had been going beforehand.

Attica quickly put her shoes on, grabbed the bag with the gold stones and ran to catch up with the man.

"Where are we going?" she asked.

"My brother has just confirmed my suspicions. I know where to find those creatures now."

They walked for about an hour until the ground started to grow soggy, turning the cracked earth into a muddy mire that made progress difficult.

The Bird Man told her that in the centre of this vast expanse was the Marsh of Malgoxo, a cursed land for animals in Nigrofe, who only went there to die.

"The cornolombrigas are afraid of my brothers and sisters," said the Bird Man. The girl was perplexed by this way he had of referring to the scorpions. "So I had a pretty good idea they'd be hiding out in the most isolated place in Nigrofe, far away from the monastery and pilgrimage routes."

"Pilgrimage routes?" asked Attica a little breathlessly. She was finding it increasingly difficult to keep up with him.

"My brothers and sisters go on a pilgrimage to Venquinta every three hundred and fifty-eight years, coinciding with the arrival of the one that rests."

This didn't exactly help to clarify the girl's state of mind, but she preferred not to ask any more questions, since the answers would only confuse her even more.

The Marsh of Malgoxo absorbed all the light from the high ceiling of Nigrofe. It was a gloomy, disturbing place, and Attica felt her heart shrinking as they neared its borders.

The stagnant waters emitted stinking puffs of sulphur. A few twisted, ugly plants grew on its surface, on which the army of insects flying over the lake would alight from time to time.

"There they are!" exclaimed the Bird Man with satisfaction.

Attica could see dozens of elongated creatures like snakes swimming around in circles on top of the water. They had brown bodies with black spots, round, white eyes and two little horns on their heads, between which sprouted a couple of slimy tufts of hair.

The masked man entered the marsh and headed in their direction. The water went up to his waist. The cornolombrigas fled as soon as they detected the intruder's presence, except for one that swept over the dirty liquid to meet him.

Attica felt this shrill voice inside her head, something like a hidden echo that came from the deepest part of her being.

"What do you want with us?" asked the voice.

"You know very well what I want!" answered the Bird Man. "Where are Dinis and Vinicius? Where are those delinquents hiding?"

"Our nature forbids us to reveal this kind of information. We are only messengers, not traitors."

The Bird Man lifted his hand, and the cornolombriga rose from the water, hovering in the dense air of the marsh. Attica heard a desperate shout inside her head, which caused her great pain and made her fall on her knees. She realized what was happening: the Bird Man was torturing the cornolombriga.

"Leave it alone!" she demanded, getting to her feet.

A second shout echoed around the corners of her head as the elongated creature writhed in the air. Attica ran towards the aggressor and barged into his back with all her strength. The Bird Man, however, didn't move an inch. He slowly turned around to face her and banged her on the head with his stick.

The marshy landscape started spinning and a flash of pain shot through her head. In the end, she fell down on the watery surface, unconscious■

Zancamaza

12	king prawns
2	skinned chicken breasts
250	grams of spicy chorizo
200	grams of smoked streaky bacon
4	handfuls of rice
¾	litre of chicken stock
3	tomatoes
1	onion
½	red pepper
1	green pepper
2	chillies
	hot cayenne, garlic powder,
	black pepper, oregano, dried thyme,
	1 clove of garlic, 2 bay leaves, oil

Chop the chicken breasts and the spicy chorizo in small pieces. Cut the streaky bacon in little cubes. Cut finely the onion, the green and red peppers and the tomato. Peel and crush the clove of garlic. Wash the king prawns. Heat a drop of oil in a saucepan that can be covered. In the oil, fry the chicken breasts and the chorizo. When they start to turn golden, add the streaky bacon.

When everything turns golden, add the onion, peppers, a pinch of ground black pepper, the chilli, ¼ teaspoon of garlic powder, ½ teaspoon of hot cayenne, ½ teaspoon of oregano and ½ teaspoon of dried thyme. Let the mixture cook for five minutes, stirring all the time to prevent it sticking.

Add the chopped tomato, the garlic, chicken stock and bay leaves. Wash and strain the rice and add it to the saucepan when the stock starts to boil. Cover the saucepan and let it boil for ten minutes.

After this time, place the king prawns on the rice without peeling them, cover the saucepan again and let the rice cook for another ten minutes.

I imagined that staying quiet would suffice for Mastrina Xaoven to continue her narrative long enough that I wouldn't have to play the klavia, but I was wrong.

"It's a quarter of an hour after the start of your lesson," declared my teacher, who in the course of Attica and Fuco's adventures had regained her place in the rocking chair.

I tried to convince her to go on with the story a little more, but to no avail. I did, however, get her to make a promise: if I made an effort with the instrument and she was "reasonably satisfied," then we could continue with the adventure over dinner, so long, needless to say, as I got my parents' permission to return home later.

I sat down at the klavia and, having warmed my fingers with a few routine exercises, played as well as I could one of the pieces I'd learned over the preceding months. Months! Whoever would have thought such a thing the first time I made the trip to this house! If Attica's story was just a ruse to acquaint me with Gwende music, then I had to admit it was highly effective, albeit the path was a tortuous and slightly-exaggerated one.

In the end, we carried on the lesson for another quarter of an hour to make up for the time we'd lost at the beginning. I phoned home from the hallway. My brother answered and played the fool for a while before going to get my mother. She wasn't exactly overjoyed at the thought of me returning to Fundete after nightfall, but when I promised to take a taxi, this ended up smoothing things over.

I went to the kitchen, where Mastrina had already started preparing our dinner.

"We're going to cook zancamaza," she told me. "It's a typical Zambelan dish. Take an onion from the fridge and chop it finely on this board."

I did what she'd asked. The onion put up a good fight against the knife strokes by filling my eyes with tears. When I got to the stage where I couldn't see anymore, Mastrina took over from me.

"The trick is to open your mouth wide and to breathe through it while cutting."

"But then I'd look like a complete idiot," I protested, washing my eyes at the sink.

"That's why it's always better to cook on your own," laughed the old woman.

She gave me another task: to wash and chop the tomatoes and place them in a large, white bowl. The work was simple enough, though it was also dull and monotonous. It became much easier when Mastrina took up her narrative again.

To begin with, she felt a distant beating in a hidden part of her head, which slowly came closer, accompanied by this unbearable pain. She then started remembering, and her body was paralyzed by an irrational fear. She thought about the cornolombriga writhing in the air and shouting out in agony.

She opened her eyes and discovered a surface bathed in greenish light moving to the rhythm of some rapid footsteps. She realized what was going on: the Bird Man was carrying her like a sack over his shoulder. Her hands were tied by a rope, from which hung the bag of gold stones.

A warm, viscous liquid ran down her face. She stuck out her tongue and confirmed her suspicions: it was blood, a consequence of the brutal blow with the stick that had knocked her out. That would explain the terrible throbbing in her head.

Attica wriggled about on the man's shoulder, and he dropped her on the ground. It was then she saw the impressive landscape opening out before them. They were in the middle of a vast plain surrounded by a chain of craggy mountains. The wind swept over the plain, whistling violently. She was horrified to see that the ground was completely covered in scorpions, except for a circular space at the centre of which she and her abductor were walking. Unlike in Bragunde or the rest of Nigrofe, the arachnids here were not heading in a single direction in long lines, but seething and jostling about in a veritable sea of insects.

In front of them, some powerful walls enclosed a town made up of hundreds of small, thatched houses that ascended the side of a hill in an orderly fashion. At the summit, like a colossus overlooking the whole valley, was an imposing, square building whose walls were peppered with multiple windows.

"Venquinta Monastery," said the Bird Man out loud.

A shiver ran down the girl's spine. In pain, her clothes still wet, she realized she was not in a good state.

"Do you know why you're still alive, new friend?" asked the voice behind the mask. Attica shook her head. "Because you are the key for me to get to the brothers."

"I've never even met them," she replied drily.

"Yes, but they're waiting for you – or at least for the gold contained in that bag."

The Bird Man squatted down beside her. Attica could see her own reflection in the red crystals of his eyes. She had an ugly wound on her forehead covered in a black scab that mingled with her hair.

"Those ruffians are hiding in the monastery's catacombs," said the little man, the tip of his white beak close to the girl's nose. "I have searched all over Nigrofe, and it turns out they were hiding at the very centre, where nobody would bother to look for them. I'm not surprised they managed to dupe old Touro, that much is normal. But I swallowed their bait as well and for that I congratulate them."

"I don't know what all your wrangles have to do with me."

"Your role is simple, new friend, you will get those two little mice to come out of their hole. They know about the blind man's gold, they reached an agreement with him by means of the cornolombrigas. When they open the door to the place where they're hiding, that will be my moment."

The pain inside the girl's head increased and relaxed its intensity cyclically, like waves kissing a beach. In addition to this, she occasionally felt dizzy, and a strange taste of rust had affixed itself to her palate.

"I saw the way you treated the cornolombriga. I'm not going to help you mistreat anybody else."

"You think I tortured that thing for pleasure? Had it not been necessary, I wouldn't have wasted a single second of my time on those repugnant creatures. But I'm not going to discuss morals with you. You have to accept that helping me is your only alternative, unless you really don't value your life or that of the children who were with you."

"You can't do them any harm. They're far away from here," ventured the girl, though she wasn't all that convinced.

"Are you sure you want to test me?" The threatening tone of the question increased her sense of unease. "Do what I say, and nobody will suffer."

Attica fell silent in acceptance of her defeat. The Bird Man lifted her up again and headed towards the town walls. As they walked along, a large corridor free of scorpions opened out before them.

The city gates were open and led to a paved street that climbed towards the monastery. Branching off the street were numerous alleyways, like the tributaries of a river. On either side, small, stone houses were lined up in long rows. As they passed through the town, they didn't encounter a single living being. In fact, there weren't even any scorpions, which seemed to respect the sacred enclosure of Venquinta.

The gate to the enormous building of the monastery was also open. A long corridor led to the cloister, which surrounded a large, inner courtyard divided into four parts by a cross of gravel. Ornamental plants grew in each of the four quarters. In the centre of the courtyard was a tall, metal column crowned by a sphere with four clocks. Attica realized this was Dinis and Vinicius's mechanism, the one Cecilio had told them about on that distant night in Bragunde.

The huge mass of the monks' residence rested on the columns of the colonnade. In between its singular walls, the only sound that could be heard was the tireless whining of the wind. And yet, despite her uncomfortable position, Attica couldn't shake off the feeling they were being watched from the windows of the cells.

The Bird Man's boots crushed the gravel of the path as it crossed the courtyard and entered one of the doors leading inside the building. It then traversed a maze of high-ceilinged corridors until petering out in the kitchen. Behind the chimney, hidden by a large, black cauldron, a small door led to some narrow stairs that smelled of damp. The masked man set Attica on the ground and ordered her to go forwards. As she descended the steep steps, a distant rumour gradually increased in intensity until it turned into the jovial atmosphere of a swinging party.

The stairs led to a corridor that was lit by several torches on the walls. The man pointed to a door at the far end.

"Your time has come, new friend. Remember what's at stake and don't do anything stupid," he said, untying her hands.

Attica went along the corridor, carrying the bag with the gold stones. Shouts and songs filtered through the door and mingled with the monotonous drip-drop of beads of moisture on the ground.

The metal door was all rusty. Attica knocked very loudly, and the metallic boom echoed along the corridor. Nobody answered, so she decided to try again. At the third attempt, a small, sliding window opened, and she could make out a pair of black eyes gazing out at her.

"Yes?" a man's hoarse voice could be heard over the sound of partying.

"I'm here to see Dinis and Vinicius."

"Dinner and victuals?"

"No, Dinis and Vinicius!"

"I don't know what you're talking about, girl. Go back to your cell before somebody catches you rolling around the catacombs."

And without further ado he shut the little window in her face.

Attica looked back and discerned the threatening figure of the Bird Man watching her every movement in the darkness.

"How the hell did I ever get into this mess?" muttered the girl under her breath. "That's the last time I listen to hicupé…"

She banged on the iron door and, a short while later, the same pair of eyes peered through the gap.

"You again? Didn't I tell you…?"

Attica took some gold stones out of the bag and handed them to the man through the window.

"Tell the brothers I have the blind man's gold. They'll understand."

The man silently took Dendria's seeds, gazing at their texture in amazement.

"Wait just a moment," he said.

Shortly afterwards, the metal door opened, and a blast of sweet wine hit Attica in the face. The man led her along another corridor to a large, square cellar. There, sitting around a table, five revellers formed a tuneless choir that sang:

I was born in the distant north,
in the south I have my home,
I live in the sultry west
and in the east will pass away.

It didn't take Attica long to realize they were drunk. The one who'd opened the door staggered over to a stool and deposited his bottom there with a thump. He then grabbed a jug full of wine and gulped it down, spilling a large part of the contents on his long, black beard.

Four of the men looked like monks and wore thick, brown tunics that were tied at the waist with a rope.

The attire of the other two, on the other hand, was very gaudy and consisted of baggy, sky-blue, silken trousers, white shirts with floppy sleeves and waistcoats embroidered in all the colours of the rainbow. They each wore a cylindrical, red hat on their head, which was topped by a black tassel. These two extravagant men were almost identical, so Attica decided to address them directly.

"Are you Dinis and Vinicius?"

"Who's asking?" said one of them.

"My name is Attica. I've brought Cecilio's gold so you will activate the obelisk. You need to hurry because..."

"Wait just a moment, what obelisk are you talking about?" stammered the one who looked more drunk, while a monk spewed a cascade of red wine on the floor.

"Our obelisk, you fool!" his brother rebuked him. "What other obelisk would it be?"

"Oh, our one!" said the drunk man before his head landed with a crash on the table. A few seconds later, he was snoring deeply.

The other brother staggered to his feet and laid his hand on Attica's shoulder.

"He can't take his drink," he admitted. "But sit down, sit down! My name is Dinis, and that good-for-nothing is my brother, Vinicius. Why don't you join us and tuck into some food?"

"There's no time! You have to leave this basement and activate the obelisk!"

"You look like an intelligent girl, Attica. Do you really think a rusty thing like that is going to keep Tartarus away? That was just a ruse to deprive Touro of his money. And we would have succeeded, had this womanizer not fallen prey to his appetite..."

The girl stared at him with a mixture of rage and astonishment.

"You damn liars!" she exclaimed. "Do you know how many people risked their lives because of your little trick?"

"Those lives were lost anyway, girl. The only thing that's left is to await our cruel destiny, and we're in the perfect place to do that – the finest pantry in all Nigrofe! We have enough wine and food to last us for ages!"

The extravagant man pointed to the walls of the cellar. One was occupied by the largest barrels Attica had ever seen. Another two were covered in shelves that rose to the ceiling and were full of imperishable foodstuffs in glass jars. On the last remaining wall were large, wooden chests possibly used for the storage of salted meat and fish.

Attica was just about to fly into a rage again when the Bird Man made his appearance in the cellar. The monks leaped up from their seats and, with all the difficulty of their drunken state, prostrated themselves on the floor before this formidable figure.

The joy on Dinis's face went out and was replaced by a slight, melancholy smile. With a pat on the neck, he woke his brother, who stood up, knocking over his stool, and walked slowly backwards.

"Here are the lamentable causes of my anxiety!" thundered the Bird Man, pointing his stick at them.

The brothers glanced at each other and fell on the masked man in a last, desperate act of bravery. Their rival pushed them back with a thrust of his stick, crushing them violently against the shelves, from which a deluge of jars fell and smashed on the floor. Directed by the stick, Dinis and Vinicius began to climb the wall, the skin on their faces slowly turning purple. Attica understood the Bird Man was strangling them, just as he'd tortured the cornolombriga in the Marsh of Malgoxo.

She tried to come to their aid, but a movement of the aggressor's hand stopped her in her tracks. With tears in her eyes, she watched as the breath slowly abandoned the bodies of the brothers, who'd already given up the impulse to fight.

The mask's red eyes were then turned towards her.

"Liar!" roared the girl, but that was the last word she uttered. She felt her throat being compressed so the air couldn't get through. Attica closed her eyes and resigned herself to her fate■

"Now you'll have to forgive this old woman who needs to go to bed," said Mastrina as she cleared the plates from the table and, having emptied the leftovers in the bin, placed them in the sink.

"You're a marvel at keeping an eye on the time, I have to admit," I said resignedly, getting up from the table as well.

My teacher accompanied me to the door, where we took our leave of each other with a kiss on the cheek. Outside, it had just started to drizzle.

Alert in Audierna Due to Flooding of River Ioke

Newspaper staff

The alert owing to the floods that have overwhelmed the south, east and west of Audierna in the rainiest autumn of the last two hundred and fifty years has reached the doors of the capital.

The Environmental Agency issued sixteen warnings of "danger of death" and recommended the evacuation of hundreds of homes in fear that the River Ioke might flood as it passes through Plugufan and Linne.

The desperate situation being experienced in the nabrallo of Zambela, in the south-west of the city, has spread to other parts of central Audierna, forcing the deployment of additional SAN units, which, with their teams of amphibian vehicles, have been preventing acts of pillage.

The peace was short-lived. A brutal storm shook Audierna that weekend. At nightfall on Friday, the sky was filled with hail-laden clouds that hours later unleashed heavy downpours on the streets. Every autumn of my childhood, I had endured the rain and the whims of the thermometer, but I'd never seen such gusts of wind as those that destroyed roofs and cracked sturdy trees like they were toothpicks. The waters of the river rose as far as Decature Street, flooding the lower part of Plugufan.

On Saturday, the grey clouds settled over the large Ioke valley, uniting earth and sky in a violent collision of electric sparks followed by noisy claps of thunder that absorbed the usual sounds of life for a period of two days.

On Monday, classes were suspended because of the damage caused by the storm. On Tuesday, once the storm had abated, I was obliged to go back to school. Even so, the wind continued blustering hysterically, with no fixed abode, directing the rain like a drunken shepherd and making it impossible to use an umbrella.

So it was that, two months after the first time, I appeared in Mastrina Xaoven's porch, again soaked to the skin and with my umbrella a mass of twisted steel. The old woman emitted an almost inaudible greeting when she opened the door and then went to the bathroom in search of a towel, which she handed to me. She then headed towards the stairs. Her climbing the first step became such a painful struggle that I ended up seizing her arm in order to help her.

Upstairs, she sat in the rocking chair and covered her legs with the red blanket. I grabbed the stool and sat down beside her. We stared at each other with silence the only word between us. My gaze conveyed the compassion I felt for her.

"Is it so bad?" she asked.

"Tell me, what did you do this weekend? I remember leaving you on Thursday in perfect condition."

"You know, the crazy things we young people get up to…"

Outside, the rain slid down the misty windows of the balcony. The oil heater kept the room warm. I was grateful to be dry inside that refuge.

"How's it going with Nivardo?" she asked abruptly.

"I can't believe you still remember his name!"

"Nor can I, to tell the truth," she smiled. "It's a pretty name."

"It's an old man's name," I said without thinking. "It's not going at all, we both do our own thing."

The hammering of the hail was the only sound in the room. I analyzed the best way to spit out the question that was lodged inside my throat.

"You said some time ago you were married," I managed at last. Mastrina nodded. "What happened? Did he…?"

"He didn't die, if that's what you mean. It just didn't work out. That's all."

My silence invited her to continue.

"We were very young, a couple of striplings really. I got pregnant soon after we were married, but the child was never born. This miscarriage led to the diagnosis of my disease. Otherwise, I would have died a long time ago, no doubt, so I could say I owe my life to that unborn child. After that, everything went pear-shaped. I couldn't give you a single reason. I suppose it was all for the best. He got married again and had several children. The last time I heard about him was in the papers, when he retired from the chair of history at Verrenorde."

"And weren't there… any others?"

"What is this, an interrogation?" she protested, feeling a little embarrassed. "Of course there were! But nothing serious. For decades, pain wore the skin of my anxieties in praise of this cruel inheritance. My marriage, my work, the child I lost… even my love affairs! All my life has been conditioned by the frailty of my health."

Her little eyes glistened, lost in time and memory, like two flames on the verge of going out. Her lower lip trembled nervously, and her fingers, twisted by arthritis, folded over and formed two fists.

"Guiomar, do you mind if we postpone today's lesson?"

"Not at all."

"I should have said something before. I thought I would be better, but I feel far too weak, and my body is crying out for bed. Of course, we'll make up the time as soon as possible."

"Don't worry."

I wasn't in a hurry to go back home, which would have meant shutting myself in my bedroom to do my homework, so I helped Mastrina to go down to the bathroom, where she took her medication. I then accompanied her to the bedroom and, although she kept insisting I leave, helped her to lie down. She got into bed with her dressing gown and socks, but was still shivering from the cold for quite a while.

I sat at the foot of the bed and rubbed her feet on top of the cover. The old woman positioned the pillow against the bedhead, sat up and leaned against it.

"Do you want us to continue the story?" she asked.

"It's not necessary, Mastrina," I replied very generously, though in truth I was dying to get back to Nigrofe.

"Come on, just a bit. As long as my strength lasts."

The vision of the cellar dissolved into a thick mist until something suddenly altered the irrevocable sequence: Saturn's three sons burst in from the corridor, each brandishing a glass bottle with a burning cloth in the neck. They smashed the bottles at the feet of the Bird Man, setting fire to his coat.

A shrill cry, as of a wounded animal, came out from under the mask. The lively flames enveloped the small body of the man, who wandered desperately around the cellar, trying to remove his coat. Attica felt the pressure on her throat subsiding, allowing her to breathe once more. Little by little, she recovered her clarity of vision and was able to admire Fuco's speedy arrival on the scene. The boy was carrying a stick with a ball of burning cloth at the end, which he thrust into the opening of the Bird Man's beak. He then ordered his companions:

"Get Attica!"

The Bird Man tried to pull the burning cloth out of his beak, but the thickness of his gloves prevented him from doing this.

Xes and Zeno grabbed the girl under the arms and dragged her to the corridor. The monks, confused by what was going on, got up from the ground and fled the cellar as well, as the fire began to spread dangerously to the furniture. The last to get out were Prisco and Fuco, who slammed the metal door shut behind them.

Fuco knelt down next to his friend, who was sitting on the floor, trying to catch her breath.

"How did you make it past the sea of scorpions?" asked Attica when she'd regained the ability to articulate sounds.

The boy took out the peach stone Cecilio had given him.

"See this? Well, it appears to repel the insects. I'll give you the details later. Right now, we have to get out of here."

He reached out his hand to help Attica to her feet, but she rejected his offer.

"Dinis and Vinicius!" she shouted. "You have to get them out of there!"

"You must be kidding! That cellar's burning like hell itself," replied Fuco angrily.

"That's precisely why we have to help them. We can't just let them die there."

"Oh shit!" screamed the boy before taking off his shoes, hitching up his trousers and heading back to the burning cellar.

He came out a while later, dragging the body of the Bird Man, who appeared to be unconscious. He'd finally managed to remove his coat, and the rest of his clothes were severely burned. Prisco, Xes and Zeno took a couple of steps backwards when they saw him, driven by fear.

"I couldn't see the brothers," said the boy. "An enormous curtain of fire only let me go in a couple of yards. But I did manage to catch this little trout near the door. Tell me, do you believe I'm a firewalker now?"

"You're crazy, that's what you are!" Attica rebuked him. "What on earth made you rescue this murderer?"

"I had no choice," explained Fuco. "He's the murderer, not me. Besides, we still don't know what to do. With the twins gone, this crook is the only one who can shed some light on the Great Evil threatening Audierna."

Attica fell silent. She knew her companion was right. She got up with Prisco's help, and they legged it out of the catacombs. Having retraced their steps, they reached the cloister, where they caught their breath, surrounded by the magnificence of the architectural structure.

They gazed at the Bird Man lying on the ground with his white beak resting on his chest and his clothes still smouldering.

"Who's going to do it?" asked Fuco. The three brothers instinctively moved away from the body, ruling themselves out of the task.

Attica went over to the supine figure and very carefully stretched out her hand to take the beak. Trembling with fear, she pulled off the mask to reveal the Bird Man's real face.

The first thing that surprised the expectant travellers was the discovery that behind this macabre mask was not a man, but a girl of about eleven or twelve. She had regained consciousness, but her eyelids still covered half her large, chestnut-brown eyes, which had this deep, serious glow, far from the childish innocence they should have had. The skin on her reddened face was covered in blisters; some of her long, black hair was scorched as well.

Attica asked Fuco for the water bottle and poured a trickle of water on to the girl's scarred lips.

"I suppose you were expecting something else, new friend," stammered the girl. Without the mask, her voice no longer inspired respect or fear. "This is not an apology, but you should know I did everything for a reason. I owe allegiance to my mother, who will soon be free as a result of my actions."

"Your mother?" inquired Attica.

"Even you foreigners must have heard her name being pronounced with fear. I am Tartarus's daughter.

"Many centuries ago, the news that Dendria, the sacred tree, had been stolen spread through Nigrofe like a trail of gunpowder. That same day, a powerful quake shook the very foundations of the Green Country. Tartarus had been freed and was coming up from the abyss of Vathis. The Great Evil advanced towards Venquinta, sowing death and destruction in her wake. At that time, this was a land of monks and farmers, so the men were not equipped to deal with such a threat. The monks shut themselves up in the monastery in horror, ready to pray for the return of the tree, which would balance the two forces again.

"The poor farmers, seeing they'd been abandoned by those who'd previously controlled their destiny, decided to confront Tartarus. They put their children inside the monastery walls and, armed with sickles and scythes, waited on the plain of Venquinta for the giant to arrive. It was a complete and utter disaster. Despite their best efforts, the men were systematically crushed by that superior being.

"But then something happened that would change the course of history until today. Tartarus was not alone. On her back, she was carrying a baby, the first baby she'd had in Vathis, which was growing while waiting for Tartarus to shed her skin. Unfortunately, this event happened during the battle, causing the baby to slide off its mother's back down to the ground. The farmers of Nigrofe, in desperation, directed all their anger at the creature and killed it.

"Seeing the body of her only child lying lifeless on the plain of Venquinta, Tartarus swore she would not rest until she had wiped all trace of humankind from Nigrofe. First, she headed towards the monastery. I was just a little girl by the name of Calandra, with the same appearance I have now. With my human parents fighting against the impossible, I'd remained inside the walls, looking after my little brother. And yet obedience was not one of the traits of my previous character. Disobeying the orders I'd been given, I abandoned my brother and approached the city gate out of curiosity. As I passed through the entrance, I came face to face with the colossal Tartarus, who stopped in order to fix me with her eternal gaze. I could feel the mixture of hatred and sadness exuded by her presence in my body. Taking care not to hurt me, she lifted me on to her back as a way of making up for her lost child. She then went back to the abyss of Vathis.

"For three hundred and fifty-eight years, I lived on my new mother's back, turning into her first guest and participating in the suffering she experienced. Every day, I learned from her wisdom and absorbed some of her power. When it came time to shed her skin, the Great Evil returned to Venquinta, depositing me in the exact same place where the farmers had previously killed her child. The monks, who during my stay in the abyss had been studying events, offered Tartarus a new guest, another girl. The Great Evil accepted the offering, placing the girl on her back and withdrawing again to Vathis. Thus continued the cycle of her pain, in which my beloved mother was trapped in the memory of her loss.

"After my liberation, I took shelter in the Grove of Coenobio, at the foot of the mountains that surround Venquinta. There I lived completely apart from the world of humans, surpassing generations without growing old. Every time my mother released one of my siblings, after the shedding of her skin, I would collect the child and kill it. This way, I avoided them having to endure the sad existence I had been living in ever since my abandonment. I often thought of going back to Vathis, but not even with all the power I'd inherited from my mother could I go down to that immeasurable abyss.

"One day, not many years ago, as I was wandering around the woods, I discovered a crack in the ground, which had been revealed by a chestnut tree falling over after an intense storm. I got into the crack and came across a strange figure lying in the shadows, dressed in this outfit with its face protected by this mask. These clothes hid the skeleton of the original Bird Man.

"Down in that dark cavity, I had an idea. I put on the outfit and went to speak to Colonel Touro. Helped by the revered memory of the first Bird Man and by the powers I'd inherited from my mother, I had no problem getting that stupid governor to act according to my wishes. His low intelligence acted in favour of my interests. I convinced him I'd had a dream, a revelation in which I'd been forewarned of the upcoming birth of one who was to kill him and take his place as leader of Nigrofe. As a means of preventing this fateful destiny, I suggested he shut up all the women inside the monastery. Touro, overcome by his fear, did exactly this.

"This enabled me to prevent any other children being born, so at the next shedding of the skin there would be no replacement to offer as guest. Finally my mother would break her cycle of suffering! Finally her terrible power would be released!

"But an unexpected event interrupted my carefully-laid plans. Two mysterious foreigners arrived in Venquinta. Nobody had ever heard of them or knew where they'd come from. They said their names were Dinis and Vinicius. They offered Touro their services to install a mechanism that would keep Tartarus away forever, forcing her to live confined in Vathis and prolonging her anxiety without end. Well, I'm glad to say that today I've been able to rectify that mistake."

Attica thought about Dinis's confession in the cellar. The obelisk that rose proudly in the middle of the monastery courtyard was nothing but a useless piece of junk, a trick to hoodwink Touro. Calandra continued her story, her voice growing ever weaker.

"It's time for the shedding of her skin. As every three hundred and fifty-eight years, the arrival of pilgrims from all over the world, my good brothers and sisters, anticipates the coming of the Great Evil. Touro's soldiers and the townsmen, realizing this was going to happen, ran away and took refuge on the other side of the mountains days ago. You thought you could defeat me with fire? Quite the opposite! My mission is complete, and victory is near."

The five stayed still when the girl finished her discourse, which contained a dark, threatening note. Every word that came out of her mouth was a battering ram against the defences of their courage, plunging them into a terror so deep they felt as if they were trapped in a nightmare. Attica eventually broke the silence.

"What... what does this Tartarus look like?" she asked.

At that precise moment, a powerful tremor shook the walls of Venquinta, causing rubble to fall from on high. When she heard this brutal vibration, a fearful smile of satisfaction spread across Calandra's childish face.

"You'll soon find out, new friend■"

Burrowing scorpions live mostly underground in holes they themselves have made. They only leave their holes to hunt and reproduce. They are exclusively nocturnal. They're capable of surviving without food for a very long time, sometimes even years, since their resting metabolic rate hardly requires energy.

The young are kept on their backs and fed with a liquid that is secreted through the dermis. During this time, the female displays aggressive behaviour.

Faculty of Biology (UoV)

The landscape had turned ashen, having absorbed the humidity of a week-long storm that had downed trees and street lamps on the pavements of Fundete and, on the cement of the avenues, created large lakes whose skin was ruffled by the wind. It was a very strange autumn, full of comings and goings that made it difficult to predict the arrival of winter.

At dusk on Wednesday, it was still bucketing down, and the eaves gutter was insufficient to carry off so much water. Gusts of hail were beating furiously against my bedroom window when in the distance, downstairs, the sound of the phone disturbed the monotony of the evening.

Minutes later, there was a knock at the door of my room. It was my mother.

"You know who that was?" she asked from the doorway. I shook my head, sitting on the bed with my science book resting on my thighs. "Mastrina Xaoven. She has health problems again, so you won't have a lesson tomorrow either. You can use that time to study."

I looked down and carried on reading, without hiding my sadness at the news.

Later, over dinner, my parents weighed up the possibility of getting me a new teacher. I was down in the dumps at the time and didn't protest against their decision. Perhaps because I thought it was reasonable enough or any protest on my part would be futile.

On Saturday, the four members of my family gathered together. My father had spent the whole morning in the kitchen, preparing his estokuise. Everybody congratulated him on the dish, including me, though as always it was just a little too salty for my taste. What could you say to someone who so evidently enjoyed preparing the meal?

After lunch, we collapsed on the sofa to watch an old comedy full of love and intrigue. It didn't take my father long to fall asleep, while my mother concentrated on knitting a sweater for a cousin who lived in Linne. My brother, meanwhile, grabbed a comic from the rack and started to read. In the end, I was the only one paying any attention to this corny film I'd already seen more than a dozen times.

I felt all itchy. There was no way I was capable of staying where I was! I got stealthily to my feet and crept up to my bedroom, put on my boots, found a long overcoat and tied a scarf around my neck. Not knowing how to justify my escape, I decided to present it as a fait accompli.

"Mum, I'm just going for a walk," I said without even going into the living room, poking my head around the door.

My mother took her small glasses off her nose and placed them on the side table.

"We have to get changed in an hour. Your father has some tickets for the opera."

"For the opera?" I asked in dismay.

"Yes, for the opera. And don't adopt that bored expression. We haven't been for months."

"That must be the reason for all the existential angst I feel. My hormones go haywire whenever too much time passes without my listening to a bunch of fat people howling into the wind."

"Ha, ha, ha. You can make as much fun as you like, but I want you here showered and dressed in an hour."

I went down to Plugufan, sheltering from the rain in the arcades of that quarter's long streets. A light was on in the kitchen of the old house, and a shadow was bustling about behind the curtain. This was a good sign, or at least so I thought until Mastrina's brother opened the door. He was wearing a dark suit, which made an amusing contrast to the flowery apron protecting his front.

"Good afternoon," I greeted him in surprise. "I wanted to see Mastrina Xaoven, is she at home?"

"Are you Guiomar?" asked the man in response. His smile revealed a perfectly-white set of teeth.

"Yes, I am," I confirmed while entering the dark hallway.

"My sister is right, you look a lot like her when she was young," he remarked in astonishment.

"Well, she never said anything to me..."

"She's in the bedroom, why don't you go and see her? Meanwhile, if you'll forgive me, I'm going to carry on washing the dishes."

I walked towards the door of Mastrina's bedroom, which was ajar. I knocked and opened the door a little more. The room was dark, except for a stream of light that filtered through the curtains. A strong smell of almond cream hung in the heavy atmosphere.

"May I come in?" I asked.

"Turn on the light," replied a frail voice from the shadows.

The lamp on the ceiling revealed the ravages of the disease. Looking tiny against the whiteness of the pillow, Mastrina's face was a gesture of pain framed by her loose hair. A pair of round, metal glasses perched on her nose.

"Do you always sleep with your glasses on?"

"It's so I can see in my dreams."

I sat down on the bed. The old woman followed my every movement with her eyes, not moving her head.

"I have a favour to ask," she confessed. "I've been playing the tune from Pistorum's *Summer Sketch* in my head all morning. Could you put on the record?"

"The question is to find it!"

"Oh, don't worry, second shelf from the bottom, on the left."

I ran to the klavia room. Following her instructions, I soon located the record she was after. I placed it on the turntable and turned the volume up high so she could hear it downstairs. I went to the bathroom to get a hairbrush from the wicker basket and then returned to the bedroom.

The sad music of the hicupé filled the house. It started with some weary, nostalgic notes on the klavia, which were soon followed by the sweet sound of a flotorne. An almost inaudible set of drums marked out the rhythm and completed the whole.

I placed Mastrina's pillow in such a way that she could sit up. The old woman closed her eyes to listen to the music better. In the kitchen, her brother continued doing the dishes. I took a lock of her hair and started combing it with the brush, trying to avoid pulling on any knots.

"I spent the whole night in hospital," she informed me. I carried on combing, unsure what to say. "The illness is getting worse, and they've had to increase my medication. That said, I don't know what's worse, this medication leaves me feeling exhausted. On the bedside table is a piece of paper with the address and telephone number of an ex-pupil of mine. He is extremely talented, and I understand he's recently started giving lessons. That's something I'm going to find difficult from now on."

"Just when I was getting used to you…"

I took another lock of hair and carefully combed out the knots.

"Mastrina, are you afraid?"

The old woman stretched out her hand and placed it on mine, trying to give it a squeeze. She was frozen.

"I'm terrified," she confessed without losing her smile. "But it's not all bad news. Guess who paid me part of what I was owed."

"The music magazine?"

"Can you believe it? Better late than never. Next month, they're going to publish the first part of my monograph."

The record finished, and I got up to go and turn it over. Mastrina asked me to stay with her.

"I've heard the bit I was interested in. Carry on combing my hair, please. Now it's my turn to do the talking."

The earth shook periodically as if a giant were playing at hammering the foundations of the world. Attica and Fuco, followed by Saturn's three sons, left the agonizing Calandra lying on the stones of the cloister and headed down the long corridor towards the exit of the monastery. From there, they could see the vast plain that spread out in front of the hill, embraced by a ring of mountains whose tops were tinged by the greenish glow of Nigrofe's light.

They waited expectantly, every blow sending a shiver down their spines. Barely a couple of minutes later, an enormous shadow appeared between two of the peaks.

At this point, a chorus of desperate screams broke the tense silence of the place. All the women of Nigrofe, confined in the monastery cells, were pleading to be freed, while hundreds of arms stuck out through the barred windows.

"What shall we do?" asked Fuco. His face had gone absolutely pale.

"We have to get them out of there!" exclaimed Attica.

The five ran back into the monastery. As they were entering the corridor that led to the cloister, Prisco ground to a halt and pointed to a windowless room on one side that was closed by an iron gate.

"Look at that! There are various bunches of keys on those hooks. They must be the keys to the cells."

Fuco pushed at the gate.

"Blast, it's locked!"

"Wait just a moment!" said Xes before zooming off in the direction of the courtyard. He returned a short while later, out of breath, carrying a broom in his hand. "I saw this earlier in the kitchen."

The boy dried the palms of his hands on his trousers. Then, very carefully, he introduced the broom handle through the iron grating and retrieved each of the bunches of keys. Attica piled them together on the ground and knelt down beside them.

"There are ten key rings, and each has a number. If you look at the rows of windows, the monastery also has ten floors."

She distributed two sets of keys to each person, keeping one pair for herself.

"Get them all down into the courtyard!" she ordered. "Good luck!"

They ran along the maze of corridors until finding a staircase that led to the upper floors of the monastery. Zeno remained on the second floor, Xes on the fourth, Prisco on the sixth and Fuco on the eighth, while Attica carried on climbing until she got to the top floors.

Each key ring held about forty keys, so it wasn't exactly a simple task to open all the doors. Inside each of the enormous cells, they came across the same pitiful scene: dozens of women divided according to age, huddled up and hungry, barefoot and dressed in nothing more than white, linen nightdresses. There were some bunks against the walls, but these were not enough for so many people, who lay on the cold flagstones to rest.

It took them almost two hours to free everybody. When Attica arrived back in the courtyard at the head of her last group, the oldest women, she found it impossible to locate her colleagues in all that bustle of bones and white cloths. Some of them were crying, hugging relatives or friends they hadn't seen in years. Others were shouting out names, hoping their desperate calls would be answered. The majority just wept in solitude, their features distorted by fear, yelling in panic whenever another blow shook the ground.

Attica finally managed to make out Prisco and Fuco among the sea of heads.

"Where are your brothers?" she asked Saturn's son.

"They're still opening cells."

Attica rubbed the back of her neck, wondering what to do. Warm, smelly sweat soaked her back and armpits.

"Let's have a look to see what's happening."

The three children passed through the mass of bodies to the exit. Many of the women were pleading for help, while others thanked them. There were even some who reproached them for getting them out of their cells and leaving them out in the open.

Outside the monastery, there was a semblance of calm. The tremors had ceased, and the sea of scorpions was strangely quiet. They went down the hill, through the deserted town of Venquinta, towards the city walls. At the gate, they stealthily climbed the steps of a staircase that led to the upper part of that impressive wall. There, they found the enormous siege engines that were aimed threateningly outwards, between the gaps in the battlements. They crept up to one of these weapons and crouched down to glimpse what was going on outside.

That was when they first saw Tartarus, the Great Evil, lying in front of the city gate, surrounded by her army of pilgrims.

Tartarus was a gigantic scorpion with a shiny, crimson body and eight yellow legs. At the front, she had two powerful pincers, and her elongated tail ended in a sharp, black stinger.

Next to her was a boy of about ten or eleven, probably her most recent guest. He was totally naked, sitting on the ground with his head between his knees.

A voice suddenly filled the silence of the plain. The children pressed against the stone wall to see Calandra, who was dragging herself painfully towards Tartarus.

"You're free, dear mother, you're free!" she shouted as loud as her damaged lungs allowed.

Tartarus stretched her yellow legs, lifting her body off the ground and raising her tail in the air in attack position. With a rapid movement, which the children perceived as a reddish bolt of lightning, the huge insect stuck the point of her stinger in Calandra's chest, silencing the girl's cries once and for all.

The Great Evil started to glow, as if a light were emanating from inside her body, and the terrified spectators could detect her anger. Tartarus had just realized no offering was waiting for her, and this filled her with rage. She made up her mind to destroy the sacred Subteran enclosure stone by stone. With a violent blow of her tail, she opened a crack in the thick wall, which succumbed to her power as if it were made of paper.

Attica grabbed her colleagues by the clothes, tugging at them to rouse them from the paralyzed state they were in. They ran like crazy until reaching the monastery out of breath. At the entrance to the large courtyard, Zeno and Xes were waiting impatiently for them.

"What's going on?" they said in chorus. Tremors continued to shake the ground, and roofs collapsed in a cloud of rubble. Some of the columns in the cloister began to crack, causing the women gathered there to cry out even louder. As if this were not enough, the fire in the cellar had spread and affected one of the wings of the enormous building.

They were cornered. Try as she might to rack her brains, Attica couldn't come up with a useful thought that would help them in this difficult situation.

"We're in a real mess," she said to Fuco.

"I have an idea," replied the boy, his face deathly pale. "Hold on to this."

He handed Attica the last of Dendria's seeds, which he'd kept in his pocket ever since Cecilio entrusted it to him. He then headed for the exit, disappearing through the sea of women.

Attica remained rooted to the spot, gazing at the humble peach stone she held on the palm of her hand. Suddenly a terrifying idea exploded inside her head.

"Noooooooooooo!"

Her shout rose above the general hubbub. Prisco ran towards her, chasing her through the trembling bodies that filled the courtyard. Attica was pushing her way through, trying to go as fast as possible. They abandoned the cloister and ran under the high ceiling of the corridor that led to the entrance. They passed outside and came face to face with the image of Tartarus, who had stopped her ascent of the hill about a hundred yards from the monastery. Fuco was standing in front of her. The large scorpion aimed her stinger at the child, taking him by his woollen jersey. She then lifted him gently through the air and placed him on her back.

Attica raced towards the monster, ignoring Prisco's pleas to stop. When Tartarus saw her, she stretched her legs and lifted her deadly stinger into attack mode. But this didn't discourage the girl, who carried on desperately advancing, waving the peach stone in her hand in an instinctive gesture of rage. The Great Evil perceived the presence of Dendria, and her body began to emit a blinding light that illuminated the hillside with all the force of a star.

A powerful vibration rocked the territory of Nigrofe. Tartarus was afraid. Not just that – she was petrified by the sudden appearance of her enemy's seed. She decided to flee. She turned around and raced away over the devastated ruins of the town.

Attica and Prisco ran after her, but when they reached the walls of Venquinta, the colossal scorpion's shadow was already disappearing behind the mountains. The girl fell down on her knees and screamed in pain. Prisco fell down beside her, hugging her close and trying to calm her down■

HICUPÉ: FROM THE NABRALLO TO PLUGUFAN

Mtna. A. Xaoven

Hicupé in the Bragunde dialect, or hic-cup in the Zambelan, is a musical genre that arose at the end of the last century, whose origins are disputed by the Malluma nabrallos of Bragunde and Zambela.

Hicupé reached the height of its popularity in the first half of this century, when it succeeded in breaking through the borders of the nabrallos and entering the Gwende part of Audierna – in particular, the district of Plugufan – where it gained a healthy number of fans, despite the prohibition to listen to it on the part of the confederal authorities. This musical genre is characterized by a very strong rhythm, a tendency towards improvisation and a constant invitation to dance, which, among the most exalted dancers, can come close to a trance.

SATURN MAGAZINE OF MUSICAL STUDIES

"Damn, that's not possible!" It was forty minutes after the time I'd promised to be home. Attica's story had completely absorbed me, and I was still coming to terms with poor Fuco's fate when I happened to glance at the clock on the bedside table. "My mother's going to kill me, she's going to kill me!"

The first thing it occurred to me to do was to phone home from Mastrina's hallway, though my family was probably already on the way to the opera. What a fine mess!

"Was there something you had to do?" asked Mastrina Xaoven, seeing my worried expression.

"There was! My father got some tickets for the opera, and I'm late. I should have been home a long time ago."

"Oh, I'm sorry, Guiomar."

"Don't be. It's just my mother's nonsense, she's crazy about hobnobbing with Audierna high society. None of my family really likes going to the opera!" This outburst of sincerity made the old woman laugh. "I'll put up with the deluge when it comes, there's no point worrying about it now."

Mastrina's brother entered the bedroom. He was holding – a little perilously, it must be said – a tray on which he carried two cups, a smoking teapot and a plate with various pieces of cisté.

"Tea time!" he announced enthusiastically. "Guiomar, will you make some room on that table so I can put this down? The cisté isn't like the one Attica makes, but at least it's fresh. I bought it this morning from a bakery on Decature Street. By the way, they're still cleaning up all the mud from the flood."

Having deposited the tray, he filled one of the cups with tea and offered it to me. I accepted politely, but Mastrina quickly came to my aid.

"Go on, put that cup down!" She then addressed her brother, "Guiomar is not a fan of infusions."

"Oh dear!" exclaimed the disappointed waiter. "Is there something else you'd like?"

"No, thank you. A piece of cisté will be quite enough."

"Well, I'm in the kitchen," said the man before retiring. "If you need anything, just give a shout."

Mastrina drank her tea thoughtfully, in small sips. I dived into my helping of cake.

"Your brother's very kind," I remarked.

"He most certainly is," agreed Mastrina. "A real treasure."

A gust of thick hail fell on top of the old house. The savage hammering of the tiles filled everything. Mastrina's trembling hands put the cup back down on the tray. She sank her head into the pillow and smothered a groan with her eyes closed.

"Are you OK?" I asked in concern. The old woman silently shook her head.

I jumped off the bed and raced towards the kitchen.

"Mastrina's not well," I informed her brother.

The man wiped his hands on a cloth and accompanied me to the bedroom. I remained in the doorway, watching the tall, thin man sit down next to his sister and stroke her hair.

"Are you in pain?" he whispered. Mastrina nodded. When she opened her eyes, a tear slid down her cheek. "Don't worry, poppet. I'll go for a painkiller."

He staggered to the bathroom and quickly returned with a white pill in his hand, which he gently introduced into the patient's mouth. He then lifted the cup of tea to her lips, and she took a sip. The old woman closed her eyes and sank back into the pillow. I exchanged looks with her brother.

"I'd better let her rest," I murmured from the doorway.

"Sit down here," said Mastrina in a frail voice. "I only need a couple of minutes."

I replaced her brother on the bed and sat down next to her. The man left the bedroom, pausing in the doorway to observe the scene with a look of concern.

"If she needs anything else, please let me know," he said before returning to the kitchen.

The effect of the painkiller was soon visible on the old woman's face, and she gradually abandoned her rigid gesture of pain. Barely five minutes after that, she took my hand. I could feel her skin was frozen and realized she was trembling with cold.

"Where were we?" she asked.

Attica's bitter sobs descended into a bout of nervous hiccups. Prisco carried on holding her close, though all attempts to calm her down were in vain. Zeno and Xes soon joined them. They realized what had happened when they saw the traumatic state the girl was in and opted not to ask any questions.

The prisoners slowly filed out of the monastery, and some

groups of women wandered aimlessly along the town's devastated streets.

"We have to go after him!" shouted Attica suddenly, rising to her feet. "We have to go and find him!"

"That's impossible," replied Prisco, trying to restore a little serenity. "You heard the Bird Man. Even with all her power, she couldn't go down to Vathis. How do you think we're going to do it?"

"You defeated him! With your ingenuity and bravery, you conquered the fearsome Bird Man! Are you going to turn into cowards now?"

"It's not a question of cowardice, Attica," intervened Zeno. "We're not even talking of confronting Tartarus on our own, it's just that we wouldn't even make it down into the abyss."

"Then I'll go on my own. I'm not going to abandon Fuco. He sacrificed himself for us!"

"I don't think Fuco did this so that you would then commit suicide in Vathis," remarked Prisco, giving her a serious look.

In a fit of rage, the girl ran away from the brothers and violently punched the stone wall, hurting her hand in the process. She then shouted out with all her might before collapsing on the ground in defeat.

As the hours went by, things calmed down in Venquinta. The scorpions had disappeared, and some of the women had started organizing their return to their homes, since they came from all four corners of Nigrofe. For their part, the men had come down from their refuges in the mountains and had even created the first clean-up brigades as a step towards the reconstruction of the town.

Their actions in freeing the women had given Saturn's sons the aura of heroes, which legitimized each and every one of their decisions. Owing to the absence of any authority, the brothers agreed that Zeno would take charge of the work of defending the town. Colonel Touro's army would be back soon, and the people of Venquinta were not prepared just to let him retake power. This decision met with the initial opposition of the monks, who were determined to regain the dominance they'd lost when Touro took over Nigrofe. The women's firm support for Zeno, however, soon put paid to that conflict.

For his part, Xes was in charge of organizing meals. Since all the foodstuffs in the monastery's cellar had been lost in the fire, he had to make use of the stores in the town itself, which, while modest, would be enough to endure the likely siege by Touro's army, so long as this wasn't too lengthy. Xes was helped in all these tasks by a team of five people. Cooking for so many people was a massive job, but the boy coped admirably well.

The general atmosphere was one of joy and optimism, but these feelings didn't permeate through to Attica. An old healing woman had treated the hand she'd wounded in her fit of rage against the wall, and it hardly hurt anymore. But she was overwhelmed by a terrible sense of sadness. Fuco's memory gnawed away at her insides. However hard she tried, she couldn't get the image of his capture out of her mind. The girl spent hours sitting on top of the thick city walls, gazing at the place where Tartarus's shadow had disappeared, that shadow that was carrying her friend, her companion, the one who'd sacrificed his existence so that they could live.

"You have to eat and rest," said Prisco on one of his visits to the top of the wall. He was the only brother who hadn't been allotted a specific role, and he bustled about, helping out wherever he could. "Whatever your road is going to be, you'll need all the strength you can get."

It was with this mysterious sentence that he managed to persuade the girl to follow his advice. Attica came down from the wall and passed through the crowd of people that filled the town. She felt like an intruder in the midst of all that vibrant joviality. How different was this image of Venquinta to the one she'd seen the first time, when she was being carried like a sack of potatoes on the Bird Man's back! Farmers, blacksmiths, craftsmen, monks... all engaged in a chaotic machine that was bent on slowly repairing the damage caused by the Great Evil.

She looked for Xes in the stores, three enormous, wooden sheds with large doors and no windows, propped against the great city walls. She found him inside one of them, piling up sacks of cereals. The boy smiled when he saw her, believing perhaps that she'd decided to throw off her mourning. She asked for something to eat, so he gave her a loaf of bread, some cold meat, fruit and a large jug of milk. She retired to the open field that surrounded the monastery complex on top of the hill. There, she prepared to swallow unhurriedly, so as not to punish her stomach too much, which was unused to food after so many hours of fasting. It wasn't easy. The sudden awareness of her hunger made her want to devour, to gobble down, everything that Xes had placed at her disposal. After eating, she lay down on the grass, covering herself with her coat. It didn't take her long to fall asleep.

When she awoke, she noticed a thick blanket of mist advancing from the north, which ended up plunging Venquinta into a magical, emerald night. She felt better, as if various tons of weight had just been lifted from her shoulders. She went down to the houses. The haze had not only diminished the light coming from Nigrofe's high ceiling, it had also quietened the lively atmosphere in town. It seemed people were using this opportunity to rest after all the frenetic activity of the last few hours. She headed back towards the food stores. Along the way, the only people she met were a young couple walking along, holding hands and enjoying the tranquillity of the alleys. With the blessing of the girl responsible for keeping an eye on the food, she filled a rucksack with various tins of food, some bread and cold meat, and a wineskin full of water.

She then headed for the gate in the city walls. As she exited the gate, the two guards on duty bowed their heads, allowing her to pass without asking any questions at all. She was quite a celebrity. She'd even gained a reputation as a witch among some of the men who'd come down from the mountains, owing mainly to her air of introspection and her strange, blond hair.

Attica walked in the same direction Tartarus had taken before disappearing behind the mountains. On the plain, the mist was even thicker, and she could barely see a couple of feet in front of her. All around her was absolute silence. And yet she couldn't shake off the irrational sensation that she was being followed. I'm becoming paranoid, she thought. That would hardly have been surprising, given the succession of dangers she'd lived through in recent times.

After she'd walked for several hours, the plain suddenly gave way to a territory that was dotted with sharp rocks. She took the path that wound its way through this forest of crags. The girl's breath and the echo of her footsteps were the only sounds in that place until she suddenly heard some rocks crumbling behind her. She quickly turned her head, but all she could see was more silence. She waited a couple of moments, trying uselessly to glimpse something in the mist. Then she continued her journey.

The path came to an end at an enormous wall of rock that was steep and had almost no jutting edges. She had finally arrived at the mountain chain that enclosed the plain of Venquinta. She reached out and felt for the best place to start climbing, eventually opting for a vertical vein made up of a lighter mineral. Several little plants grew there, and the surface had one or two cracks she could hold on to.

Having gulped down some water, she started climbing the enormous rock face. She had barely gone a couple of metres when her right foot slipped out of the crack where she'd put it. She tried to grab hold of a bush, but the plant's spindly roots gave way beneath her weight, and the girl ended up falling into the void.

She was just expecting to be on the receiving end of a hefty bump when some arms reached out to break her fall. As a result of the impact, Attica and her unexpected saviour both rolled on the ground.

"So you were planning to go down to the abyss of Vathis all on your own?" said a familiar voice.

"Prisco!" shouted Attica, feeling both happy and surprised. "Were you the one following me?"

The boy sat on the ground and pulled down one of his woollen socks to reveal his calf, which he'd scratched against a stone.

"I could see in your look that, however many sensible reasons we gave you, nothing was going to deflect you from your course. So I decided to keep a close eye on you."

"If you're here to try and persuade me to go back, then you can..."

"Hey, stop right there! I'm not here to persuade you to do anything. I tried that in Venquinta and failed. I'm here, for example, to inform you that five hundred feet to the east is

Coves Pass, a much easier route through these mountains."

Attica sat down too and shook the dust off her coat. She then gazed for a moment at Prisco: the orange tuft, the large head, the ridiculous clothes... His brothers knew exactly what they wanted. He, however, seemed to let himself be carried along by the current of life. Without great aspirations, but always giving the best of himself in whatever he did.

"Are you coming too, then?" asked the girl.

"I am – if you don't mind."

"Of course I don't! I'm going to need all the help I can get..."

Prisco pulled his sock up to his knee. He then jumped up and helped Attica to her feet.

"My brothers have found their roles in these crucial times we're living in, but I have not," he said solemnly. "I know they'll be disappointed when they find out we've left. Especially Zeno, who was counting on our help to defend the town. This journey, going to Vathis to confront the Great Evil... is absolute madness. Though Fuco's actions were even madder, weren't they?"

"They sure were!" replied Attica, smiling. "We're all indebted to him."

"Promise me one thing. If we return..." The boy swallowed with difficulty when he uttered these words, "you'll come to see my father with me and tell him all about our adventures. Maybe then he'll stop thinking we're just a bunch of layabouts."

The boy's request made Attica burst out laughing, something she couldn't remember doing.

"I promise you we'll go and visit old Saturn, and Fuco will come with us," she said, holding out her hand. Prisco shook it firmly, thereby sealing their pact.

They then started walking to the east, alongside the mountains, in search of Coves Pass, avoiding the sharp rocks that stuck out of the ground like a primitive monster's canines.

The boy went ahead, marking out the route. As she followed him, Attica made an effort to think about Fuco, in her mind's eye drawing his swarthy face, his snub nose and the gap between his front teeth that detracted from his smile. This intrepid youngster had sacrificed his existence so that she could live. His heroism had weakened an illness that lurked in the deepest parts of that unknown land, an evil that would come back in the future to destroy everything if they didn't do something to stop it.

She felt in the pocket of her coat for Dendria's last stone and squeezed it tight. Her eyes misting over with emotion, she rushed to catch up with Prisco■

And that was as far as Mastrina's strength lasted that day. I took my leave of her with an affectionate kiss on the cheek. Her brother accompanied me to the front door. As I emerged on the street, a grey drizzle was falling on Plugufan. My mood was tinged with melancholy, as if Attica's emotion and my teacher's aches and pains had infiltrated my spirit. I walked thoughtfully up 15 August Avenue, ignoring the droplets of water. Back at home, I shut myself in my room. My family had yet to get back from the opera, so the reprimand on account of my disappearance would have to wait. I didn't mind. After all, it wasn't so important.

My parents decided not to get me a new klavia teacher. According to them, this would enable me to focus on my studies. And that is what I did. Without maila training or visits to the old quarter, time was something I had more than enough of. Miraculously, I got the necessary marks and passed the year, which came as quite a surprise.

After that most recent visit, I didn't go back to Plugufan for a couple of days. On Thursday, after leaving school, I retraced my usual route. It was a cold, sunny afternoon at the end of autumn. I felt nervous without knowing why. I took a deep breath before turning the corner of the old ironmonger's. Mastrina Xaoven's little house looked weak and vulnerable. The blue shutters covered the windows, and someone had pruned the old oak, cutting off the thickest branches. I pressed the front doorbell without expecting any response. Nobody answered. I circled the house to the back garden. The ground was bespeckled with dark oranges that rotted in the tall grass. The bench where I'd once fallen asleep had disappeared. The back door was locked, of course.

After that day, I went back to Mastrina's house from time to time, always getting the same dispiriting reply. On the last of my visits, I found out from a neighbour that my teacher had moved to live with her brother in Goibe, a distant town in the north. I was a little annoyed she'd gone off like that, without saying goodbye. But I promised myself I'd go and visit her when the summer relieved me of my academic obligations.

And that is what I did, though the account of that trip is kept in another of the boxes piled up in my apartment. It was undoubtedly a pleasant coincidence to come across Mastrina's story again after all that time.

ARCTA – one of the mouths in Nigrofe's roof, which gives rise to icy gusts.

AUDIERNA – may refer to: 1. a city formed by the districts of Linne, Fundete, Plugufan and Seina, to which must be added the Residential Complexes of the North, the Gwende colonies south of the River Ioke, and the Malluma nabrallos of Zambela and Bragunde; 2. the confederal republic whose capital is the city of the same name, with an area of 1,995.4 km^2 and a population of approximately 9,100,000 inhabitants (Audernians). This calculation does not include the population inside the city's nabrallos or the other Malluma settlements distributed throughout the confederal territory.

BRAGUNDE – a nabrallo located in the south-east of Audierna, bordering the Gwende colonies to the north and the nabrallo of Zambela to the west.

BRUN – a term used by the Gwende community to refer to the Malluma community, which the latter considers offensive.

CHIELA-EBENAXO – Nigrofe's roof, also known as "the inner sky," made up of a green material that is capable of emitting a light that illuminates the vast cavity.

CHIONA – a term used by the Malluma community to refer to the Gwende community, which the latter considers offensive.

CISTÉ – a traditional Gwende dessert consisting mainly of almonds and flour. It is usually eaten with hot chocolate during the seasons of autumn and winter.

COENOBIO – a mythological grove located in Nigrofe, beyond the belt of mountains that surrounds the plain of Venquinta.

CORNOLOMBRIGAS – fantastical beings that live in Nigrofe and act as messengers.

Coves – a pass through the mountains that surround the plain of Venquinta, in Nigrofe.

Dendria – a sacred peach tree that forms part of Malluma mythology, one of the symbols of the Subteran cult.

Estokuise – a Gwende stew consisting of hare meat seasoned with oil, wine or vinegar, garlic, onions and various herbs, all placed raw in a well-covered vessel that is then cooked on a low heat.

Flavacocos – mythological animals in Nigrofe, which look like giant cockerels with yellow feathers.

Flotorne – a metal musical instrument, a kind of large malgrine.

Fundete – a residential district of the city of Audierna, located to the north of Plugufan. Also known as Upper District.

Goibe – a Gwende town located in the north of the Confederation of Audierna.

Gwebraae – a Gwende culinary speciality made with various garden vegetables and native to the region of Kervengare (in the west of the Confederation).

Gwende – an ethnic group from the north that settled mainly in the northern part of Audierna. The Gwendes wield political power throughout the territory of the Confederation.

Hic-cup – see *hicupé*.

Hicupé – a term in the Bragunde dialect that is used to refer to a musical genre with Malluma origins, which in the Zambelan dialect is called *hic-cup*.

Hodepunke – at 3,776 m., Mount Hodepunke is the highest peak in Audierna. It is located just to the west of the capital and, on a clear day, can be seen from the district of Linne. Hodepunke is a composite volcano.

Ioke – the river that crosses Audierna from west to east.

Klavia – a musical instrument made up of a group of keys that, when pressed with the fingers, activate a mechanism that beats against metal strings, creating different sounds.

Kuepere – a bush in the genus *Cydonia*, about three metres in height, with numerous branches and oval, green leaves. Its fruit is eaten either baked or stewed.

Likeur – an alcoholic drink typical of the district of Plugufan, made from the fermentation of peaches.

Linne – a district located in the far west of the city of Audierna and seat of the state's political institutions.

Litenklave – a wind instrument made up of a single-reed mouthpiece and a tube formed by various pieces of wood with holes.

Maila – a game that confronts two teams of sixteen players each. It is played with an elliptical ball on an oval pitch. The main objective is to score more points than the other team by kicking the ball between the posts of the opponents' goal. Players can pass or run with the ball. This game is known for its physical contact, in which a player may be brought down to prevent an attack.

Malgoxo – a marsh in the fantastical land of Nigrofe, located in the centre of a desert.

Malgrine – a wind instrument consisting of a long, metal tube that gets wider from the mouthpiece to the bell and produces a variety of sounds according to the force with which air is propelled through it.

Malluma – of, pertaining to, or characteristic of the people who inhabited Audierna before the Gwende conquest.

Malnovan Logo – the sacred book of the Subteran cult, part of Malluma culture.

Mastrino/a – a form of respectful address used to refer to outstanding figures in the field of art or academia.

Migas – a person with a Malluma as one parent and a Gwende as the other.

Motlave – a string instrument, the largest and deepest-toned of its family, usually played with one end resting on the floor.

Nabrallo – each of the ghettoes created by Law 77/19/57 for the exclusive use of Audierna's Malluma community.

Nigrofe – also known as "the Green Country," the name of a territory in Malluma mythology. It is located inside an enormous cavity.

Paarine – a tree in the genus *Pyrus*, whose height varies between two and ten metres, depending on the variety. It has a straight, smooth trunk and a well-developed crown. Its fruit is edible.

Pilco – a game between two teams of nine players each, very popular in the nabrallos, the aim of which is to get an elliptical ball through a ring according to a fixed set of rules, the most important of which is that it cannot touch the arms.

Plugufan – the oldest district in Audierna, located on the central riverbank of the River Ioke. It was the first Gwende enclave in these parts.

Puna – a mythical plague that swept across Audierna many years ago, origin of the legend of Nigrofe.

SAN – the Special Agency for the Nabrallos (SAN) is a section of the Audierna police force whose role it is to keep order in the Malluma nabrallos. SAN agents have been accused of sectarian or discriminatory behaviour towards Mallumas and even of collaborating with paramilitary supremacists in the committing of crimes.

Sanctapersico – a forest in Malluma mythology that once held Dendria, the sacred peach tree.

Seina – a district located in the east of the city of Audierna, the most important financial district in the Confederation.

Subteran – an ancient Malluma cult based on the various balances present in the universe.

TARTARUS – also known as "the Great Evil," a representation of wickedness in the Subteran cult.

VATHIS – an abyss in the mythological land of Nigrofe, home to Tartarus.

VENDAVAL – an islet located at the widest point of the River Ioke as it passes through Audierna, at the border between the nabrallo of Zambela and the Gwende colonies in the south. It was once used as a military prison.

VENQUINTA – a mythical, walled city in Nigrofe, seat of the monastery that bears its name. It is located in the centre of a wide plain.

VERRENORDE – seat of the University of Audierna, located in the territory that belongs to the Residential Complexes of the North.

VOLBLOEDE – also known as "ancestral blood complaint," a degenerative disease suffered by Gwende women. It normally comes to light after a miscarriage and prevents the woman from having any more children.

ZAMBELA – a nabrallo located in the south-west of Audierna, bordering the Gwende colonies to the north, the River Ioke to the west and the nabrallo of Bragunde to the east.

ZANCAMAZA – a traditional Malluma dish, the base of which is rice and the main ingredients chicken, king prawns and vegetables. It is normally seasoned with a large amount of pepper.

Read more titles in the series  published by Small Stations Press!

Andrea Maceiras, EUROPE EXPRESS

Only when I got to the hotel and observed the postcard under the magnifying glass was I fully aware of everything. Of the fact that what's happening is the greatest coincidence or most unbelievable stroke of destiny in my life and necessarily has to mean something. I can't stop gazing at this postcard, although, every time I look, a new shiver runs down my spine. I visited this city when I was still a teenager, but how could I ever have imagined I'd be here again ten years later? And how could I ever have thought I'd find them again, my old school friends, in a postcard? That summer we spent travelling around Europe was amazing, but it all ended in tragedy. At that time, winter entered our lives and never left. We barely kept in touch.

Nico is a computer programmer from Coruña in Galicia. On a business trip to the city of Bergen in Norway, he visits the quays of Bryggen, a place he has been to before. He buys a couple of postcards from a shop there and, much to his surprise, discovers that one of them has captured the moment when he and his friends visited Bergen on an Interrail trip after leaving school ten years earlier. There they all are: Óscar in his Deportivo football shirt with Bea; Nico with the slightly pretentious Mía, poring over a map; the Italian exchange student, Piero, a few feet behind them. But where is Nico's girlfriend, Aroa, and his best friend from school, Xacobe, the other two members of the group? Nico is shocked to find that they are in a corner of the postcard away from the others and are kissing. He resolves to unearth all the mystery surrounding that trip and the bitter month of September that immediately followed, when a tragedy occurred, a tragedy that split the group apart and from which no one has recovered. He will invite all his friends to a school reunion and, by gauging their reactions to the postcard, finally learn the truth of what happened.

ISBN 978-954-384-090-8

Elena Gallego Abad, DRAGAL I: THE DRAGON'S INHERITANCE

'Have a look around you, with wide open eyes. The catacombs are
not far from here, but you have to be the one to find the keys. I
shan't be able to accompany you on the last stage of your journey,
I'm getting too old for such adventures, so I must fulfil my role as
guide by getting you to come up with the correct answers. When it's
time, the result will depend on your choices. And don't forget the
search for the dragon will be worthless if you lose what matters to
you most along the way.'

The priest spoke slowly and the boy began to feel desperate.
Father Xurxo didn't seem prepared to give him the indications he
needed and impatience was gnawing away at his soul.

'Please…'

The vicar took an apple out of his pocket, wiped it on the sleeve
of his jacket and sat on a pew in the first row, gesturing to the boy
to sit down beside him.

'Have a look around you, with wide open eyes, and tell me what
you see,' he said again, biting into the fruit.

After the death of his father in a caving accident, Hadrián is
forced to move to Galicia with his mother and start at a new
school. His mother gives him a medallion that belonged to his
father, showing a dragon in a threatening posture on one side
and the same dragon incubating an egg on the other. When the
dragon's tails move, the boy realizes this is no ordinary medallion.
Meanwhile, he has noticed the stone effigy of a dragon on the
cornice of St Peter's Church, which winks at him and infiltrates his
thoughts. The boy's destiny, it seems, is to sacrifice himself so that
the dragon can come back to life after an interval of a thousand
years, during which it has been protected in the catacombs under
the church. The boy and his classmate Mónica will first have to
locate the catacombs with the help of the parish priest, Father
Xurxo, before they can ascertain whether the dragon's existence
is for real.

ISBN 978-954-384-031-1

Manuel Lourenzo González, BROTHER OF THE WIND

Do you want to know who Amrah is? Amrah is my girlfriend, the woman I shall marry when I'm old enough, my lifelong companion. But be careful, my friend: it's a secret. Only you and I know this. Your father will find out when he translates this letter, but he'll be discreet as always and not tell anybody. I can rely on that, can't I, doctor? Amrah and I wouldn't like the news getting out. Her father is the mayor of Qhissa Hanni, an influential and wealthy person. I'm not sure he'd be happy about my wanting to marry her. I shall have to set myself up in life before I get his blessing, but I'll do this for her sake. Do you want to know what she's like? Amrah has dark skin and greenish eyes, round like the moon. She has long, delicate fingers, smooth, shiny hair, and her voice is like running water. But that's enough of that! I don't want you falling in love with her as well, I have plenty of competition with the other boys in the village!

Khaled is an Iraqi boy, a member of the Koblai tribe, growing up in the village of Qhissa Hanni in the mountains of north Iraq. He has left school to look after his family's flock of sheep, but his father and the local schoolteacher think he has the makings of a writer, so they give him a notebook in which he records his aspirations, events in the village, the life of his family, his wish to own a horse which he will call 'Ahu al-Rih' or 'Brother of the Wind', his secret engagement to the mayor's daughter, Amrah, so secret that even she doesn't know about it, the time when he and a friend go frog hunting and slip a couple of frogs into the midwife's bag, causing havoc when the midwife is due to assist in the birth of Ilaisha's son... The book is presented as a series of letters which Khaled writes to the son of a European archaeologist, Dr Meira, nicknamed 'Al-Galego', who has taken up residence in the village in order to pursue his archaeological studies and because he has grown fond of the Iraqi way of life. But the invasion of the country in 2003 by the United States and its allies casts a heavy shadow over this remote village and its inhabitants, who struggle to come to terms with the issues that are at stake and who will have to draw on all their reserves of courage and strength if they are to survive. The war will bring tragedy to the village and will force Khaled to undertake a journey he has never imagined before, to the heart of the country's capital, Baghdad. This is a journey of principle, of courage over fear, of faith and friendship, of self-sacrifice, that will change Khaled's expectations forever.

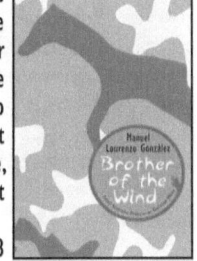

ISBN 978-954-384-074-8

Rosa Aneiros, I LOVE YOU LEO A. DESTINATION SOMEWHERE

Leo went through the security archway with far too much insecurity in her feet and restless pumping in her heart. That may be why the civil guard ordered her to take off her boots and passed the metal detector over her nervous body. Had it been able to measure her heartbeat, that little device would most probably have exploded as soon as it reached her chest. But it didn't explode, possibly because such instruments know nothing about the comings and goings of the soul. Meanwhile, the X-ray machine was closely examining the contents of her rucksack. The rucksack didn't seem exactly comfortable with its contents. It had gone from carrying sheets, folders, books and notes to holding lists of Internet addresses, descriptions in different languages, a passport, a brand-new debit card, some socks and a scarf.

After university, Leo is due to go travelling for six months with her friends Aldara, Inés and Martiño, but at the last minute her friends pull out and Leo is left to travel on her own. Her first stop, in Lisbon, Portugal, is a rain-soaked disaster. She is dragged around the city by her overbearing host and only really gets a feel for the city during the final few days, when she is cooped up in his apartment. But everything changes with her next destination, Barcelona, where she meets up with a group of friends from Latin America who call themselves 'Ruth & Co.' and busk for a living. Romance, excitement, frustration, appalling and luxurious living conditions, familiar and foreign cultures, follow as Leo travels to Granada, Córdoba, Seville and Cádiz in Andalusia, Marrakesh in Morocco and finally Istanbul. In this first instalment of Leo's travelling adventures, Leo discovers that she must learn how to leave a place before she can truly enjoy her experiences, and how travelling can bring you back full circle. She is also mystified by the graffiti that keeps appearing along her route: 'I Love You Leo A.' Who is it that has scrawled this graffiti wherever she goes, and what do they want? Only by continuing with her journey and not giving up will Leo find out the answer to this riddle!

ISBN 978-954-384-040-3

Read more Galician literature in English published by Small Stations Press!

Fiction:

Xurxo Borrazás, VICIOUS

Carlos Casares, HIS EXCELLENCY

Ledicia Costas, AN ANIMAL CALLED MIST

Álvaro Cunqueiro, FOLKS FROM HERE AND THERE

Xabier P. DoCampo, THE BOOK OF IMAGINARY JOURNEYS

Xabier P. DoCampo, WHEN THERE'S A KNOCK ON THE DOOR AT NIGHT

Miguel Anxo Fernández, A NICHE FOR MARILYN

Miguel Anxo Fernández, GREEDY FLAMES

Agustín Fernández Paz, NOTHING REALLY MATTERS IN LIFE MORE THAN LOVE

Teresa Moure, BLACK NIGHTSHADE

Miguel-Anxo Murado, ASH WEDNESDAY

Miguel-Anxo Murado, SOUNDCHECK: TALES FROM THE BALKAN CONFLICT

Xavier Queipo, KITE

Manuel Rivas, ONE MILLION COWS

Manuel Rivas, THE POTATO EATERS

Anxos Sumai, THAT'S HOW WHALES ARE BORN

Suso de Toro, POLAROID

Suso de Toro, TICK-TOCK

Poetry:

Rosalía de Castro, GALICIAN SONGS

Rosalía de Castro, NEW LEAVES

Xosé María Díaz Castro, HALOS

Celso Emilio Ferreiro, LONG NIGHT OF STONE

Pilar Pallarés, A LEOPARD AM I

Lois Pereiro, COLLECTED POEMS

Manuel Rivas, FROM UNKNOWN TO UNKNOWN

For an up-to-date list of our publications, please visit www.smallstations.com

For more information on Galician literature in English, please visit www.galicianliterature.gal